Shirley Jones and Doris Watson investigate:

The Burmese Bloodstone

Carolyn J Thomas

Introduction

Hi, my name is Shirley Jones. I am thirteen years old and live in a village called Dashington. It is a pretty little village and has a shop, a church, a school and a population of what I call, "Older than the hills and know more than the mountain brigade." It's a bit unfair really because, after saying that, most of them are nice. However, they have to know everything about each other. My Nan used to say, "What they do not know they will certainly make up," and, of course, she was right. You never told Nan she was wrong.

I live with my parents and go to secondary school, which is about nine miles away. On the whole, I enjoy school and have a best friend called Doris Watson. She is also thirteen and lives a couple of miles away. My biggest Hero of all time is Sherlock Holmes, I know he his only a fictional character, but I have always been obsessed with his logical thinking and non-emotional crime-solving talents. So maybe, (As there are "no coincidences") picking my friend Doris Ruth Watson was inevitable. She also enjoys the strange and mystical facts about the world and its universe. Together, we are a strong team and if there is a mystery of any kind, we will solve it.

This is the story of our very first case and the experiences we had to deal with.

Chapter 1 - After the wedding

It was ten o'clock at night on the first Saturday in June, two years ago. Dad, Mum, Doris and I were waiting at Philsbury railway station for a train to take us home. Dad was supposed to be driving the car home, but as Mum had put it "Dad enjoyed himself a little too much at the wedding".

So, there we were, Doris and I wearing our full bridesmaid gear, which consisted of a green velvet puffy dress with matching shoes and handbags. We looked dreadful. Dad had been calling me Kermit all day and it was no longer funny. He was pacing up and down the platform and Mum was sitting on one of the metal benches reading the "Order of Service" leaflet that we had from the church. Every now and then she would burst into song and smile.

How embarrassing, I thought, and I said to Doris "I really hope nobody from school comes to get on the train, imagine the teasing we would get at school on Monday"

"Yes, how awful it would be," replied Doris.

At last, the train approached. We could see the lights and I hoped it would hurry up, thankfully, as we got on, we could see that it was completely empty.

"Phew, that was a stroke of luck," Doris uttered under her breath.

On the train we sat opposite Dad and Mum, they were busy chatting about all those long-lost relatives. You know, the ones you only see at weddings and funerals and insist on you calling them aunt or uncle, even though you have not got a clue who they are.

Dad was hysterically laughing about the so-called comedian at the wedding who was there to entertain us all. Doris and I thought he was rubbish; we could not understand any of his jokes or what he was trying to say. But some of the guests were loving it and I saw Mum blush a few times.

"He was far too near." laughed Grandad.

Too near to what, I thought?

And to finish it all off Nan said, "He had died on stage."

This clearly was not true because Doris and I had watched him getting into a taxi and disappear down the drive. There was no mystery there. He did not appear on the stage for his second half.

It was my cousin Evie's wedding. She was an only child and she was ten years older than me. She had always treated me like a little sister and, of course, Doris was always around. So, it came as quite a shock when last year she went on holiday to America and met the lovely Kevin Richman. He lived in Kansas in America and nobody seemed to know anything about him. On the occasions that I met him, he seemed fine but a little moody, one minute he was the life and soul of the party, the next time he would hardly speak to anyone.

Oh well. Evie's choice. The engagement had been quick and the actual wedding even quicker.

At last, the train pulled into Heathbury station; this was about a ten-minute walk from home.

Success, there was not a soul on the station platform and we walked out onto the street. Everywhere looked deserted, thank goodness.

We hurried on up the lane and could see the one street lamp that was lighting up the whole of Dashington village.

We turned the corner and passed the local garage, just then Dad said "Right girls, I will race you home."

"What? In these dresses, you must be joking!" I replied, but Dad took off anyway.

We sped up a little but we could not move very fast owing to high heels. Dad had arrived at our front door about a minute before us and was shuffling in his suit pockets, looking for the front door key. Mum slowly arrived, handing Dad the key, which she had safely in her handbag. We all went inside and Dad switched on the light in the hallway.

The first job for Doris and I was to get out of said puffy dresses and so we went up to my bedroom.

Mum shouted up the stairs "Do you two want some hot chocolate? And remember to hang up your bridesmaid dresses properly in case you should want to wear them again."

"I don't think so," I said to Doris and we flung them on the floor laughing hysterically at the prospect of ever wearing them again.

We put on our pyjamas and headed back downstairs for our drinks.

Dad had put on the television and was sitting on the sofa trying to find something to watch, Mum was searching in the cupboard drawer looking for her own wedding album.

At last, she had found it and sat between Doris and me. We looked at it out of politeness, we had seen it quite a lot of times already and then made our excuses for bed.

"Why do Mums always reminisce?" I said to Doris.

"My Mum is exactly the same. Maybe we will be the same when we get older," Doris replied.

"I hope not" I replied, knowing secretly, that we probably would be.

We got into bed with our hot chocolate and talked for a long time about the day we'd had.

We had both enjoyed being in the spotlight and sitting on the top table. I was chief bridesmaid and Doris was the other one. It was strange because there was no friends or family of Kevin's there. I think his best man had been enlisted from a pub that he had been in recently.

Evie had looked beautiful; her dress was elegant and made of white lace. Her long, red hair hung over her shoulders, underneath the tiny veil she'd had. Around her neck, she had worn a heart-shaped, ruby necklace. It was encased with seven diamonds and at each end of the chain were six green emeralds. It really was "to die for". Kevin, of course, had mentioned it in his wedding speech; a red heart for his love, seven diamonds for the months he had known Evie and six emeralds to signify how many children he would like and, obviously, to match our hideous bridesmaid dresses. The guests had all laughed but, I must admit, Doris and I had felt quite sick it was so mushy.

In the corner of my eye, I had noticed that Aunt Kate did not look that pleased about it either. She was Evie's mother and my Mum's sister. I thought, perhaps it was the thought of all them grandchildren running around.

"We had best get some sleep now, Doris," I said and we were soon fast asleep.

Chapter 2 - Under suspicion

"Morning, are you both awake yet? It's ten o'clock." That was Mum, shouting up the stairs.

"Morning Doris. Are you OK?" I quietly said.

"Yes, I am fine," replied Doris.

We dragged ourselves out of bed reluctantly, got dressed and went downstairs.

It was a fresh sunny morning and our breakfast had been laid out on the patio in the garden. Dad was busy cutting the grass and waved to us. Mum brought us some hot buttered toast and some fruit juice then hurried back into the kitchen.

"What's the rush Mum?" I asked.

"Don't you remember? Grandad, Gran and Aunt Kate are coming for Sunday lunch!" Mum replied.

Oh dear, I had forgotten "Not more talking about the wedding, that's all I have heard about for months." I whispered to Doris.

She laughed. "Oh, what a pity. Dad is picking me up at eleven-thirty, I am so sorry ha-ha!" Doris replied, smiling profusely.

Just then, Mum shouted from the kitchen, "Do you two fancy a walk up to the post office? It is open until twelve."

"What do you want?" I replied

"I forgot to get some cream and I think your Dad needs a newspaper," Mum instructed.

We finished our breakfasts; Mum gave us some money and off we went. As we walked past Dad, he called, "Don't forget my newspaper. Any one will do, as long as it has got the football results in it."

"OK " I replied and we walked out of the garden gate and up the road.

We walked really slowly. Neither of us seemed to have much energy. We passed all the pretty gardens and the church; the bells were ringing but there was nobody about.

Just as we turned the corner, we saw Miles Drakeford walking down the road towards us. "Morning Doris and Shirley," he said.

I waited for Doris to reply first, I knew that she quite fancied him. But there was no response from her. I looked at her and could see her mouth was opened and her jaw was going through the motions of speaking but alas, no sound.

So, I replied, "Hi Miles, what are you up to?"

He looked straight at Doris and said, "Just having some exercise, I like to keep fit."

Doris managed at long last to say "Yes, you are looking very fit indeed..."

I couldn't help a little giggle but Doris gave me a sharp nudge and her face went bright red.

"Where are you two off to?" He asked.

Doris, who had now pulled herself together, replied, "We are just going to the post office."

"I will walk with you, if you do not mind?" Miles said.

"That's fine by me," replied Doris. I did not even bother to answer; I do not think that either of them was interested in my opinion anyway.

We arrived at the Post office. It was a quaint little shop. It had a large double window, but inside the wood panelled walls made it really dark. The lighting consisted of one bulb hanging from a single piece of string just above the counter, which did not help. Outside was a wooden bench that all of the pensioners sat on after they had collected their weekly pensions to discuss all the local gossip.

Doris piped up "I will wait here with Miles."

"I bet you will," I replied and walked in.

Mrs Dukkas was standing behind the counter; she was the postmistress and had been there forever.

"Morning Mrs Dukkas," I said.

"Good morning Shirley, how did the big day go yesterday?" She replied.

"Yes, thank you, everything went really well. We all had a super day," I said.

"I am really pleased about that, but it's a shame that your car broke down and your Dad had to leave it at the Carlton Hotel. It must have stuck out like a sore thumb amongst all those Jags and Bentleys."

"It didn't breakdown, we came home on the train," I replied.

There was a long pause and then she looked up at me from the book she had been studying on the counter and uttered, "Oh I see, do you want some paracetamol then?"

"No thank you, I want a pot of cream for Mum and a newspaper for Dad, that's all," I replied.

She thought for a moment, "I presume your mother is having the family around for lunch. She will have made a trifle yesterday and wants double cream just to put on the top. It saves her a lot of time and effort; she is probably feeling a bit lazy today. I don't drink myself but I believe a few glasses of sherry can tire you out." She looked down at me smugly and continued, "Now, your Dad will want a newspaper with the football results in it," she said, handing me one from the rack. "Here we are then Shirley, this one will do, but his team lost again yesterday."

I couldn't wait to get out; I paid her the money and headed for the door. She was such a gossip.

I met Mr Dukkas in the doorway, he was carrying two big boxes and he was laughing, he always laughed. Maybe it was a nervous thing, but he laughed at funerals, churches and everywhere. You could always hear him a long time before you could see him. Which was quite handy when he was carrying big boxes around.

"Hi Shirley, I have just been talking to Doris. I believe that the newlyweds are on their way to Singapore for their honeymoon. How nice, but should Evie be travelling all that way in her condition?"

I just stared at him and he began to laugh. Before I could answer him, Mrs Dukkas interrupted and told him to put the boxes on the counter.

"Must go," I said and hurried out.

Doris was sitting on the bench by herself.

"What's happened to Miles?" I asked.

"Someone phoned him and he rushed off. Anyway, you have been ages." Doris replied.

"That's a shame," I said.

Doris gritted her teeth and said, "What is that supposed to mean?"

"Come on Doris, I know you well enough to know that you quite fancy Miles. It really is too obvious, you couldn't talk, you went weak at the knees and your face went so red I thought you were going to faint," I said. "Not much deduction needed here."

"That's rubbish, I was just hot. You always think you're so clever Shirley, you really annoy me sometimes and anyway, let's go, Dad will be picking me up soon." Doris, in a flap, replied.

When we arrived back Doris's dad had already arrived and was having a cup of tea with dad in the garden.

"Hi, Dad!" Doris shouted. She had calmed down by now. "I will go and get my stuff I won't be too long."

We said our "Goodbyes" and Mr Watson and Doris drove off.

"Have you got the cream, Shirley?" Mum asked.

"Yes, here it is, Mrs Dukkas thought that you would need double cream if the family were coming for lunch."

"Well, she is right; I have made a trifle" Mum replied.

I interrupted her, saying, "Mrs Dukkas thought that you would be feeling lazy and also she wanted to know why our car had broken down and was left at the Carlton Hotel."

"What?' Mum replied.

"I told her that we had come home on the train."

Mum was looking annoyed now and said "My goodness, that woman knows everything."

Just then Dad popped his head through the kitchen door "Do you have my newspaper? I need to see the football results before the family turn up."

"Your team has lost again" I replied.

Mum looked up over her bowl of trifle and said to Dad "Don't bother to read the paper just pop up to the post office and speak to Mrs Dukkas, it would be quicker. She seems to know everything."

Dad just glanced at her looking mystified.

"I'll explain later," she said.

Dad took his paper and went to sit in the garden.

"Shirley, could you lay the table in the dining room? Put three wine glasses out, the pretty ones with no chips in them, and three tumblers for you, Grandad and Dad. They will be collecting the car after lunch, so they cannot have wine."

"OK" I replied and carried on.

At dead on twelve o'clock Grandad, Nan and Aunt Kate arrived.

Grandad had picked Aunt Kate up; She has lived by herself for quite a while. My uncle Jim had an accident when Evie was about eleven. I did not remember him, but Evie was always talking about him and the things that they did together when she was a little girl. She had taken it really badly when he had died twelve months later. She really missed him.

Everybody sat down for lunch. It was delicious, Mum had excelled herself today.

Most of Mum's cooking is usually overcooked, but her gravy is always good. She always says, "Overcooking food stops us from having food poisoning." Dad and I always agree and has become a standard joke between us.

Lunch over, Grandad said, "We had better go and get that car. I don't want to be too late getting home, Antiques Roadshow is on later and there is an old painting on it that was thought to be worth a fortune, turns out to be worthless."

"That's not nice," said Gran.

"Only joking" he replied, but winked at me anyway and he and Dad left.

"Come on, let's go into the lounge and relax. The dishes can wait today," Mum said.

Good idea, I thought, because that was usually my job. We all sat down and relaxed.

"Are you OK, Kate? You are very quiet. I thought that you were yesterday, at the wedding. Is everything all right?" Mum asked.

"Yes, I am just tired," replied aunt Kate.

Gran, who was having none of this said, "I know you, Kate. What is worrying you?"

Aunt Kate sat up and picked up her handbag and placed it on her knee.

Everybody went quiet, she looked really serious. Ah, I thought, this is the point when we discover that Evie was indeed in 'that condition' as Mr Dukkas had so elegantly put it. Aunt Kate was going to be a grandmother. I had not told Mum about that part of the conversation I had with Mr Dukkas, Mum was already annoyed with their nosiness, so I thought it was best not to mention it.

However, I was wrong. Even geniuses get it wrong sometimes.

Aunt Kate began, "You might think that this is a bit silly, but really we know nothing about Kevin, only that he lived in Kansas, his parents died when he was young and that he has a younger sister called Veronica.

"Evie had met him in an airport in New York when she was having coffee. He shared her table, they exchanged addresses and phone numbers and then one month later he turned up on Evie's doorstep.

"Now you can say that that is romantic. But I think it's strange. He explained to me that his job was in finance and he travelled all over the world and so when he came to the U.K he just thought about Evie."

Gran looked a bit puzzled and eventually said "Look Evie is twenty-one years old. She is a sensible girl and she is very determined. Whatever you would have said - if she had made her mind up, she would not have listened anyway."

"No, I suppose you're right. But that is not all of it," said Aunt Kate.

At this point, I wanted to get my notebook out and write down the details, but I thought it might look a bit odd. When Doris and I were solving anything that intrigued us, Doris always wrote everything down in case we forgot any important points. Oh well, I would just have to listen really carefully.

Aunt Kate started to speak again, "Well, yesterday morning... You know what wedding mornings are like, there were the usual hairdressers, florists and neighbours popping in with gifts and cards. Then, about an hour before it was time to get ready, the house went really quiet. Evie had gone for a bath and I took her a cup of tea. I came downstairs, made myself a cuppa and sat down at the kitchen table.

"I must say, I was enjoying the peace, when Kevin walked in through the back door. 'What are you doing here?' I asked him. 'It is a British tradition not to see the bride before the wedding'.

"He placed his briefcase on the table and pulled out a long red box and three white envelopes and placed them in front of me. 'I haven't come to see Evie; I need your help' he said. He opened the box and inside was the necklace that Evie wore yesterday. Kevin instructed me to give it to Evie to wear with his 'love'".

"There is nothing wrong with that. And what a beautiful gift it is," Gran said.

"Yes, I know that, but my instructions were that last night after the wedding Evie would give it back to me," replied Aunt Kate. She reached into her handbag and placed the necklace on our coffee table. "Kevin asked me to discard the box, wrap the necklace in tin foil and post it in the first white envelope to an address in St Peter's Port in Guernsey. I asked him why. He replied 'I only heard a week ago that my job needs me to be in St Peter's Port for six months. So, I have rented a house there and Evie and I will go there straight from our honeymoon. It's a surprise for Evie. I can see no point in taking the necklace through customs you know what they are like. It will be safer this way. Please do not say anything to Evie. She will only get upset about not coming straight home." Aunt Kate continued, "I had no choice and agreed to do as he had said. He further instructed me to deliver the one of the other white envelopes to Evie's bank. In the last one is three tickets for me and two others to go to St Peter's Port in July. 'Bring anyone with you. Now, I must go. See you later', he said and rushed out of the door.

"I placed the envelopes in the kitchen drawer and took up the necklace for Evie, she was delighted. I said nothing about the rest of it. I did not want to ruin her big day. So, what do you think?"

There was a long silence and then Mum said, "I do see why you are concerned. And we will all miss Evie for that amount of time, but, what an adventure. Do you remember; we all went to St Peter's Port when we were young, it was a beautiful place, Kate. Have you opened the other white envelope yet?"

"Yes, I have, last night. It was a letter to the bank. Inside was a change of name certificate changing Evie's surname to Richman and a letter authorising the bank to transfer all of Evie's money into a joint account at credit Suisse bank in St Peter's Port. Remember, she had a large sum of money in her account that Jim's Mother gave to her when he died."

Mum, who had been quiet for a while, said, "It does look suspicious, but there is probably a good explanation for it. Young people these days do things a lot different than we used to."

"Yes, I know that, but obviously the signature on the transfer letter is a forgery because Evie knows nothing about going to St Peter's Port. And forgery, in whatever day we live in, is forgery," said Aunt Kate.

Gran spoke up, "Look, don't worry. The bank will check everything out and probably will get in touch with Evie before they do anything."

Just then, Dad and Grandad returned, "Wow, who's died? Everybody looks so unhappy in here. Have we missed something?" Dad said with his usual tone.

They both sat down and the story was repeated again.

I saw my chance, and asked "Aunt Kate, may I look at the necklace?"

"Of course, you can Shirley, but be very careful with it." Aunt Kate replied.

She handed it to me and I took it over to the window. Jewellery was not really my kind of thing, but it was incredibly beautiful.

I held it up to the light. The ruby heart was so clear; there wasn't a mark or scratch in it. The diamonds were so bright and sparkly. Then, I remembered reading about pure diamonds. If they were real, they could cut glass.

So, when nobody was looking, I found a spot on the window and pressed the diamonds into the glass and slid them down, pressing really hard. When I removed the necklace from the glass, it had left a deep groove. I moved away quickly before anybody noticed what I had done and placed one of Mum's pot plants in front of it.

I sat down and gave back the necklace to Aunt Kate and she put it back in her handbag.

Then, Dad stood up and said, "You do all know that the necklace is a piece of dress jewellery. It's not the real thing! And it's probably not worth much, it's not the Crown Jewels."

"What do you know about jewellery?" Mum asked Dad. As she asked, she pointed to her, rather small, engagement ring.

Dad had to admit to not knowing a lot, but he said "Why then, would Kevin ask Kate to send it in the post?

Why indeed? I thought to myself. I did not believe that it was fake either.

Dad continued "Stop worrying, the bank will check everything out just concentrate on the holiday you will be getting. Who are you taking with you?"

Mum looked at Dad and said, "Not us, you have got my new kitchen to fit."

"Oh yes," Dad replied sounding very disappointed.

Then Gran said, "Us neither, you know what I am like with water, seasick every time."

Aunt Kate thought a while and then said, "Would you like to come, Shirley? Maybe Doris could come as well if her parents don't mind?"

I looked at Dad and Mum.

"Fine by us. Just because I am not getting a holiday, does not mean you cannot have one." Dad replied

"Great sounds fun, thank you," I replied.

They all had a cup of tea and then left.

The rest of the day was filled up with homework and getting ready for school the next day.

Chapter 3 - The newspaper cutting

You know what it's like at school, after the exams. We seemed to have plenty of homework to do, but all the teachers were busy marking papers and so they sent us all to the library to read and study what we liked.

I was looking in the mystery section and Doris was flicking through old American newspapers on the computer. She had recently been doing an exam on the American economy and the Wall Street crash. She found the American newspapers really comical and so much different to ours and that is when she saw it! The paper was the Washington Post dated December last year.

"Couple walk into Madison Avenue Jewellers in New York and try on pieces of expensive jewellery and walk out without being detected.

Some of the items were hidden in a sleight of hand way and the most expensive - The Burmese Bloodstone necklace had been replaced with a paste replica.

This necklace had a large ruby heart that had been mined in Mogok in the 1950s. It was encased with the finest quality diamonds, which were complemented with emeralds.

Also missing was a Cartier cigarette box and an emerald bracelet. The value was around 5 million dollars. The jewellers had not noticed the swap for 3 days. Please see the sketch below."

Doris could not hide her excitement; she let out a loud shriek and then a big gasp.

Everybody looked in her direction and the room fell silent. Mrs Parison, the librarian asked her if she was all right.

"I am fine" Doris replied and she summoned me over to her with her little finger. "Look at this Shirley," she said and showed me the article and we studied the sketch. "It's the one, Shirley, it's a sketch of Evie's necklace."

I was shocked but I had to agree. "Take a picture of the article Doris, we will have to discuss this further," I said.

Just then, the school bell rang and we headed for the school bus. My head was reeling, it was full of shock, surprise and mystery; the three things I really loved.

Doris and I talked all the way home on the bus and I told her everything that Aunt Kate had said yesterday. Yes indeed, we had ourselves a real mystery.

Later that evening, Doris and I spent hours on Facebook discussing the possibility of the necklace.

"Maybe it's a coincidence?" said Doris.

"I don't believe in them; you should always go on your first instincts and you must admit Doris, it all seems pretty suspicious" I replied.

Doris always thinks more about things than I do. She weighs up the odds, whereas I always jump straight in. Though, I must admit, I am nearly always right.

Doris, who had thought about the situation, said, "How would the necklace get into this country then Shirley? All of the airports would have been heaving with police officers and the customs and excise units would be looking for the jewellery."

"There are always ways, Doris. Remember, the crime was not noticed for three days and Evie had met Kevin in the airport. What if he had planted it on her? Evie is no pushover, but think how charming he can be! She has told me that it was love at first sight and he had insisted on paying for her coffee and carrying her luggage. I mean, come on! Do things really happen like that? I am not convinced." I replied.

Just then, Mum shouted, "Teas out."

"I will see you tomorrow Doris, I'd better go, but keep thinking about it and not a word to anyone," I said

"See you in the morning," Doris replied.

I ran downstairs.

"What were you and Doris talking about?" Mum asked. "You have got that look in your eyes Shirley. I hope you are behaving yourselves and not interfering in things that don't concern you!"

"No, nothing like that, just talking," I replied.

Dad chirped up, "Talking about boys I expect!"

"No. Just girlie stuff, you know." I replied.

"That's exactly what I mean," Dad said, laughing.

We sat down for tea, burnt fish fingers and soggy chips.

Dad looked at his tea and, after turning the plate around several times, said, "Looks lovely. I don't know quite which angle to tackle this. Perhaps I will go to my shed and get an axe. I suppose we should be thankful it's only the fish fingers that are burnt. I will start with a soggy chip."

He winked at me, but Mum completely ignored him.

I really was not that hungry, but ate as much as I could without breaking my teeth. I did not fancy a trip to the dentist right now. I had too much to think about. Poor Mum, the old oven she had was ancient, no wonder she needed a new kitchen. I think she had it for a wedding present, but that was a long time ago.

Mum brought the teapot to the table and sat down, "Aunt Kate has been on the phone. We are going to see her at the weekend to sort out your holiday to St Peter's Port. I have spoken to Doris's parents and they have agreed that she can go with you as long as you both do as your told," she said sternly. "Doris can come to Aunt Kate's on Saturday as well."

"Great" I replied.

Later that night, in bed, I could not help feel excited about our holiday and the mystery we were going to solve. And, of course, to see Evie.

Chapter 4 - The interesting visit

We arrived at Aunt Kate's after lunch on Saturday and we chatted about how Evie was so excited about seeing us. Aunt Kate was pretty laid back as a rule and she was good fun to be with. But today, she laid down a few rules for our forthcoming holiday.

"No going anywhere on your own and always tell me where you are going ALL the time."

We both agreed and promised to follow the rules. It was a big responsibility for her after all.

"Now, me and your mother are going to have a cup of tea and some cake, but will you girls do me a favour before you have your cake. Would you pop down the street to Evie's house and pick up a teddy bear from her dressing table? I forgot it yesterday when I was collecting some other stuff that Evie wants us to take with us. It's a small grey bear holding a red velvet heart."

"OK" we replied and got the key from the sideboard.

Evie's house was only six doors down the street. When uncle Jim had been ill after his accident, he had bought Evie a house, 'To always have for the future' he had said. She had moved into it but usually lived with Aunt Kate to keep her company.

We got to the door and went in.

"I will stay here," Doris said and sat at the kitchen table.

I walked upstairs and entered Evie's bedroom. It was decorated with pink paint and on the walls were pictures that I had drawn for her when I was small. I did not remember a lot of them, but some sparked fond memories of drawing them with Evie's help.

I found the little teddy bear sitting on the dressing table. It was easy to find. Evie was like me, neither of us were into such things. I presumed it must have been a gift from Kevin.

I joined Doris downstairs and sat down. I placed the bear on the table.

Doris picked it up and looked at it and then said "How cute."

I replied, "What's cute about it? It's just a grey, furry, look-a-like bear holding a red silky heart. How tacky."

Doris smiled and placed it back on the table, "Oh, what a shame, it's got a small tear in its back." she said.

I picked it up and placed it in my coat pocket. "Come on, let's get back," I said and off we went.

We gave the bear to Aunt Kate.

"Thank you, that has saved me a walk," she said. "Now, sit down and I will bring you a piece of cake."

We did not argue about that. Doris and I seldom liked the same food, but we both loved cake.

Doris, who had been unusually quiet, suddenly asked Aunt Kate, "Where did Evie get the cute little bear from?"

Aunt Kate replied "When Evie first met Kevin at the airport, he bought it for her in a little gift shop there. It was a keepsake for her and that is why she wants us to take it with us, but it has developed a tear in its back. Evie has no idea how that happened. It must have been poor stitching."

"Oh, I see," Doris said and just glared at me.

Then my mind seemed to wake up, what was I thinking? It was so obvious that this was how the necklace had got into this country.

Mum got up from her chair and said, "Come on girls, we must go now. You will see Aunt Kate on Saturday when Dad takes you to Weymouth to catch the ferry."

We all said goodbye and got into the car. Doris and I sat in the back seat so that we could talk about the revelation of the suspicious gift.

Chapter 5 - The Holiday

At last, Saturday had arrived. I hadn't had a lot of sleep. Doris had stayed over and we talked most of the night until we had finally dropped off to sleep. We were all packed and had several warnings from Dad and Mum. You know, the usual, "no talking to strangers, no going anywhere on your own and if you happen to get lost, tell somebody."

"You mean a stranger then" I replied.

"You know what I mean Shirley, just behave yourselves."

At this point, we just agreed before we were given name and address labels to put around our necks.

At last, we got into the car and headed off. Mum was still crying and fussing and we waved as we drove around the corner.

When we arrived at Aunt Kate's she was standing on the pavement with loads of luggage.

"Should have hired a bus looking at all that luggage. You and Doris might have to sit on the roof," chirped Dad.

"Ha-ha very funny Dad" I replied.

He managed to squeeze it all in and we set off to Weymouth.

Doris and I were really excited about going on the ferry and we had already planned what we would do if the boat got into any trouble; we were both good swimmers and we would carry Aunt Kate between us.

Everything went to plan and we boarded the boat without any problems. We rushed to the top deck and Dad waited to wave us off.

"Well Doris, now for some proper investigations. Maybe it will all make sense and Kevin might be completely innocent, but I rather doubt that. Anyway, whatever happens, we will find out the truth."

The crossing was really smooth and we headed down to have a good look around the boat. It was really big and there was a gift shop and a couple of restaurants. Before we knew it, we were arriving in St Helier.

We got off the boat, Aunt Kate enlisted a porter to help with the suitcases. Doris and I had a suitcase each but ours were on wheels, so our job was easy. We followed the porter to the St Peter's Port ferry and got on.

This boat was much smaller. We bought some drinks and snacks and sat up on the deck looking at the port. The weather was perfect; the sun was shining and the sky was a bright blue with large puffy white clouds that drifted by and shone in the water. Aunt Kate, who had put on her sunglasses, was having a little snooze. Doris and I were looking over the sides when the announcement came about the warning sirens. One siren for sitting calmly, two sirens for go to your lifeboats and six sirens for abandon ship.

At last, the boat began to move and we sailed quietly out of the port. The seas were really calm and so we did not have to listen for sirens!

We arrived in St Peter's Port at about 5 o'clock, it was a very busy little port. We could see rows of little houses lining the harbour. There was a long bridge and opposite just on a hill we could see a church. It all looked really pretty.

As we were getting off Doris pointed "Look over there, it's a castle. I love castles; can we go there?" she said with great excitement.

"Of course, we can. But not today. I remember that from when we came years ago, I think it's called Castle Cornet and there is a museum inside. Your Uncle Jim loved it here, we did not think then that Evie would be living here. He would have been really envious." Aunt Kate replied.

We walked out on to a narrow gangway that led up to the harbour. In the distance, among the many people, I could see Evie waving to us as if her life depended on it. She was jumping up and down and came rushing down the walkway to meet us. Then it was all group hugs and tears from Aunt Kate.

"How are you all? I have missed you so much." Evie asked through her tears.

Aunt Kate composed herself and replied, "We are all fine, you look so well, Evie".

Evie did look good; she was wearing white trousers and a blue top. Her long red hair sparkled in the hot sun.

"Come on, let's get you all home for tea. We can do sightseeing tomorrow and I'm sure Mum will want a cup of tea," said Evie.

"You're right there, a cup of tea would be fantastic," replied Aunt Kate.

It's funny, a cup of tea seems to solve everything. It is the same at home; whatever happened or where ever we have been it is always concluded with a cup of tea.

On the right-hand side of the harbour was a large car park and about six old fashioned buses were parked up.

Doris asked, "Are those the local buses? They look ancient. I thought our school bus looked old, but that's ridiculous."

Evie laughed and said, "No Doris, they are just historical buses for the tourists. It's not that old fashioned here."

"Watch it Doris, they are just like the buses I used to go to school on," piped up Aunt Kate shaking her head.

We all laughed and helped Evie get all the luggage in the back of her car. It was a large, white 4x4 vehicle and a perfect size for all of Aunt Kate's gear.

Evie started the car and turned right over the bridge and then turned left into the town. The sea was on the left-hand side and we followed the harbour wall. On the right-hand side was a church, and a large avenue of trees; behind these were various offices and banks.

"This is the financial hub, Kevin has an office there," said Evie. "Can you see the castle? We can visit there and opposite are old tunnels containing museums. German prisoners of war built the tunnels. The Germans invaded this island and ruled it during the war. There is even an underground hospital we can visit."

"That will be great. I can't wait," uttered Doris, who really loved her history.

We carried on the road for about four miles and then Evie turned down a small lane on the left, then we arrived at some very large double gates. She reached forward and got her phone off the dashboard and entered a number into it. The metal gates slowly opened. We drove down a very impressive drive that was lined with big trees.

"This looks all very expensive," said Aunt Kate.

"Wait till you see the house then," replied Evie.

Suddenly, we had our first view of the house. It was really old and beautiful, what I could only describe as medieval, with large arched windows and a front door that was made of wood and then studded with big bolts. It looked like a castle.

Evie pulled up outside the door and said, "Well what do you think?"

Aunt Kate was speechless, that did not happen very often. Doris and I just looked at each other in amazement.

Evie, who could see the surprise on our faces, said, "It used to be a priory where monks lived, then it became a hotel and, now, it's a family house for one of Kevin's clients who is abroad at the moment."

Just then the big wooden door opened and out stepped Kevin, wearing shorts and a very flowery shirt.

"Welcome guys and welcome mothering law" he muttered and then he grabbed Aunt Kate and gave her a kiss on the cheek.

She did not reply and she looked annoyed and a bit shocked.

"Come on in. I have tea waiting for you and also someone I would like you to meet," he said.

We walked into a large stone hall and placed all of our luggage at the foot of the stairs. We looked up and saw that there was a balcony that ran around the landing. It was lit by a fantastic chandelier that hung down in the centre of the hall.

"Come into the kitchen," summoned Kevin and we followed him and Evie through a large archway to the right of the stairs.

In the room was a wooden table, well laden with food, and by the fireplace was standing a tall, young woman with jet-black, long hair.

"Nice to meet you all, I am Veronica, Kevin's sister," she said.

She spoke with a real American accent; it was a lot stronger than Kevin's.

"I live just down the road and I have a beauty salon in the town. You are all welcome to visit me. You are probably tired now, but I could work wonders on all of you. See you soon," she said loudly and then she walked out of the room and Kevin walked out with her, chatting and giggling.

"They don't look much alike, do they?" said Aunt Kate curiously.

"No, they are not alike at all. I must admit, between us, I do find her really annoying, she thinks she knows everything and is always here." replied Evie. "But never mind that now. Let's put the kettle on and get stuck into some tea."

Kevin returned and we all sat down, chatting. Doris and I were not chatting much just eating all the wonderful sandwiches and cakes that had been laid out.

Evie announced that she had got herself a job in a jeweller's shop, two days a week and was really enjoying it. "Tomorrow we will go shopping and I will show you where I work and then we will have lunch in one of the posh restaurants," said Evie.

"Sounds great". We all replied.

Kevin left the table and went upstairs.

"Come on let me show you to your bedrooms," said Evie.

Between us all, we carried the suitcases up the stairs. There was no sign of Kevin to help us. We all stood on the landing; it was more like a gallery than a balcony and it ran all around the second floor. We peered over and looked into the large hall.

"This house is really beautiful," said Doris.

"Yes, it is, but we are only here for a few more months, and I must not get too fond of it; our house in Fletcher would fit into the hall here" replied Evie.

She opened the door of Aunt Kate's bedroom. It was huge; it had a four-poster bed and a large balcony overlooking a walled garden and, further in the distance, you could see the sea.

"This is like a five-star hotel with no bills. What a good time we are all going to have" said Aunt Kate.

We moved out of this room and went into ours; it was the opposite side of the gallery. It was the same size, but no four-poster bed and no balcony, just two single beds and a sofa.

"I thought you would both like to share and it's safer without the balcony"

We agreed, it was nice anyway. We had different things on our mind. We would be looking for clues.

Evie continued, "Do your unpacking and then you can explore the house and gardens, whilst Mum and I catch up on all the gossip."

That seemed a good idea and we bounced on the beds and chose the one that we wanted to sleep in. It was lucky that we both picked different ones. Unpacking done, we rushed down the giant stairs. Kevin was on the gallery as well; he had changed and was now wearing a smart suit and tie.

"I will see you girls in the morning, I have got to meet a business client tonight." He muttered as he was rushing down the stairs behind us. He went into the kitchen and spoke to Evie and Aunt Kate. "Don't wait up" he shouted as he walked across the hall and left.

"Does he often work at nights?" asked Aunt Kate.

"Yes, very often, his clients prefer to do their financial business at home, rather than in their office I presume," replied Evie.

"What exactly does he do then?" asked Aunt Kate

"It's something to with insurance and avoiding tax, I think. I don't ask too many questions," replied Evie.

No, I thought but Doris and I will be asking loads of questions and watching every move he makes. Evie grabbed two wine glasses out of the cupboard and they both sat down.

"Now girls, you can go and explore the house and gardens. You can go anywhere you like except for Kevin's study. It's next to the library and it has a security keypad on the door, so you will not be able to get in there anyway." said Evie.

So off we went, leaving them chatting.

"Where do we start?" asked Doris.

"Let's start down here and make our way into the garden before it gets too dark," I replied.

We entered the room next to the kitchen. It was obviously the dining room. There was a large circular table with twelve chairs and a stone fireplace and there were old pictures of flowers and plants everywhere on the wall.

Doris sat down at the table, "I could just see myself eating my breakfast in here and the butler serving up my orange juice." We both laughed.

"I know what you mean, it's unreal" I replied.

There was an adjoining door that led into a wood-panelled library; there were leather-bound books all around on the shelves and soft leather chairs everywhere. The walls were covered with religious paintings of monks. Above the very old fireplace was a picture of a monk ringing a bell with a monastery behind him. Then we saw the French windows leading out into the garden.

"Let's go out there, before it gets too dark" I said.

Doris agreed. We opened the doors and strolled onto a patio.

"Wow, what a garden," said Doris.

There were flowerbeds everywhere and it smelt of a variety of herbs, some I recognised from Mum's little pots she kept on the windowsill at home. A high brick wall surrounded the whole garden and we could not see any gate. In the corner, was a stone plinth with steps leading up to a massive block of black wood. We climbed the steps and on the top was a sundial. On it was painted the sun and the moon and, around it, were Roman numerals.

"That's a funny sundial; it has two pointers on it and what are these two bars on the sides. They look like handles!" said Doris.

We both studied it and both agreed it was rather odd and very old.

Just then Evie and Aunt Kate came into the garden.

"Come on girls, it's half-past nine. You have had a busy day and we had better get to bed, we've another busy day of shopping tomorrow," said Evie.

"Can we take some books out of the library to read in bed?" asked Doris.

"Yes of course, go and pick one each," replied Evie.

We ran into the house and looked at all the books; there was not really anything that interesting, but, in the end, I chose a book about old Guernsey customs. Doris chose a book about old houses of St Peter's Port. We returned to the hall and Evie pointed to a very old, studded door

"This is Kevin's study. It used to be the monk's chapel, there is a very old alter inside," she said.

"Can we see it?" asked Doris.

"Kevin will show you tomorrow. I don't know the security code," replied Evie.

"Goodnight then," we said and headed up the stairs.

We got into our beds they were really bouncy and comfortable; on the pillow underneath the duvet there was a little packet of jelly sweets. I remembered that Evie used to buy them for me when I was small. Doris had some sweets as well, but underneath mine was a note saying, "Shirley, I really miss you and our shopping trips together, soon I will be home and we can go shopping again." I must confess that it really touched me and I so hoped that our suspicions were all wrong. I wanted Evie to be really happy; she deserved to be. She is always very kind to everybody.

Doris, who had already finished her sweets and was reading her book, suddenly piped up, "Shirley, look! This house is in my book." She reached over and showed me a picture, "See! Do you want me to read it to you?" she said.

"OK, go on then" I replied. I was glad of the distraction away from the sweets and my memories.

Sherlock Holmes would never get sentimental. What was I thinking? I must be getting tired, I thought.

Doris began, "Well, the house was an old priory for twelve monks who lived and trained here. Behind the house, was a small monastery and there was also a chapel in the building. They were a silent order and were not allowed to talk to each other. That would be hard for us to do, how would we manage?"

"You wouldn't." I replied.

Doris ignored my comment and continued "Anyway, it was said that, one day, they all vanished into thin air and, after that, nobody ever saw them again. Legend has it, that within the grounds, there is a secret tunnel and, one night, they all escaped down the tunnel, went to the sea and sailed away to other countries. It was always a mystery because they were not allowed out and the garden is surrounded by a high wall. Apparently, all the clues are hidden in the house and in a monk's bible that is supposed to be here somewhere," she looked up at me, grinning. "Oh, can we look Shirley? It will be so exciting."

"Yes, why not. But, remember what the real reason for being here is, the necklace and finding out if Kevin is a criminal" I replied.

"Yes, of course Shirley. Good night then. I will see you in the morning," said Doris. She put her book down and I knew she was busy thinking about the secret tunnel and the possibility of long-lost treasures.

Chapter 6 - Gathering clues

We woke up early; we could smell the breakfast cooking in the kitchen.

"That smells like bacon," said Doris. We got dressed quickly and rushed downstairs. Evie was at the stove and Kevin and Aunt Kate were sitting by the table, they had already finished their breakfast and were drinking coffee.

"Morning girls, are you both OK? Would you like some bacon and eggs for your breakfast or would you prefer cereal?" asked Evie.

"Bacon and eggs, please," we both replied hungrily.

I know cereal is probably healthier but it smelt so wonderful we could not resist it and, after all, we were on our holidays. We soon gobbled it up and took our milk out into the garden.

The sun was shining and we sat down on the bench watching a squirrel running up and down the trees by the sundial. It was very agile and, when it spotted us watching, it knew it had an audience. It seemed to be showing off. It would leap from one tree to another, each time it landed on a new branch it would stop and stare at us as if it was waiting for applause. It eventually ran off and Doris and I wandered towards the sundial.

Doris was trying to tell the time with the sundial, "This isn't much good. It says that the time is ten o'clock, but it's only eight o'clock, it must be for decoration only."

I agreed, mystified. It really looked very old, what was the point of it if it didn't work? How could it be so wrong?

"Come on girls, go and get yourselves ready for a day of shopping. We are walking down so put something comfortable on your feet," shouted Evie.

Our train of thought broken, we concentrated on the shopping day that was ahead of us. Doris loved shopping; I was not so keen but it would be nice to have a good look around the small town. Kevin had already left for work when we went back inside.

We got ourselves ready and set off towards the town. We slowly walked down the long drive, Aunt Kate was not very fast on her feet, but that did not matter, it was a beautiful day and there was no rush. At the end of the drive, we turned right and crossed over the road. From that side we had a good view of the sea. In the harbour were beautiful little boats and they all seemed to have different coloured sails and there were a lot of people about, getting on with their day-to-day business. It took about half an hour to reach the town and, even though it was a Sunday, must of the shops and offices seemed to be open.

Evie pointed to a small office and we could see Kevin through the window on the telephone. He waved to us.

"Who is that with him in the office?" asked Aunt Kate.

"Oh, it will be Veronica delivering coffee I expect. Her beautician's is only a few streets away and she and Kevin are very close. We will go and see her later" replied Evie.

Aunt Kate didn't say anything else, but she looked a bit puzzled.

We turned left up a hill, towards the town square. It was really pretty with baskets of flowers and bunting everywhere; in the middle of the square was a statue of a donkey and her foal.

"That's lovely, but why a donkey?" asked Aunt Kate.

"It's to signify how strong and resilient the Guernsey people are, especially during the war when they were under German occupation." replied Evie.

"That's really nice," said Doris. She seemed to love all animals and, even though it was made of stone, she couldn't help patting it as we passed by.

"Now, where are all these shops and the bargains?" asked Aunt Kate.

There were loads of small shops and Aunt Kate was in her element. My Mum always says that when they were young, she could not pass a shop without going in. Mum was right. We must have gone into about ten shops. Doris and I sat on chairs whilst Evie and Aunt Kate tried on what seemed like the entire shop. Aunt Kate bought skirts and jackets, shoes and handbags! You name it, she bought it. Evie bought some new clothes for her job.

Doris and I bought a hat each, inscribed, "I love St Peter's Port". You know, the mandatory holiday hats. We had both had enough shopping by then and could not wait to get out into the fresh air.

"Come on let's go for lunch, there is a place I have wanted to try for ages; it is just down this little alleyway," said Evie.

There were about twenty steps so Doris and I helped Aunt Kate with all her bags of shopping. At the top of the steps was an old-looking hotel; outside was the biggest looking lantern I had ever seen.

We walked in; it looked really expensive and was very busy. The sort of place that Dad would have walked straight back out of, muttering, "It's too expensive, let's get fish and chips instead."

A waiter met us as we stepped through the door; he looked directly at Evie and said, "Table for four, is it? Would you like your usual table? I will bring two extra chairs."

Evie looked really strangely at him and muttered, "Yes please."

He ushered us to a table by the window and we all sat down. Then he took all of the shopping, put all of the bags in the corner and brought us four large menus.

Evie, who had now composed herself, said, "That's funny, it's happened to me several times since I moved here. People who I have never seen before speak to me as if I know them or they know me."

"You must have a double," replied Aunt Kate and opened her menu to see what choice there was.

We chose our meals and ordered, very soon we were tucking in; it was fantastic. Three courses later and all very full, we left.

Aunt Kate insisted on paying the bill and gave the waiter a good tip for carrying all her shopping to the door.

Once outside and bagged up Evie suggested that we would go and see Veronica at her shop.

We made our way to the salon, where Veronica met us at the door. It was a small shop with about four beauty chairs in it and at the far end was a nail bar. The salon smelt of vanilla, which was very overpowering.

"Hi there, come on in and have a look around. Does anyone fancy a facial?" asked Veronica.

"Yes please," said Aunt Kate and plonked herself down on one of the chairs.

"Now, I am no miracle worker but I will try to do something with you," Veronica said to Aunt Kate.

Doris and I thought that was really funny but Aunt Kate did not look too pleased.

I thought we had better get out of the way and so I asked if we could go out into the back garden. "It's really hot in here can we go out please Aunt Kate?"

"Yes, OK then, but stay in the garden please." she replied.

We headed for the backdoor that Veronica pointed out to us with her long, green, painted nails.

The garden was long, narrow and roughly grassed over with not a flower in sight.

"This is a boring garden," said Doris and I agreed, but I had spotted an old looking building at the bottom, it looked like an old workshop.

"Come on Doris let's go look in the shed," I said. We opened the metal door; it was broken on one side and so we squeezed our way in through the other side. Inside it looked like an old studio of some kind. There were old pieces of rusty machinery everywhere, it all looked like it had not been used for a very long time. There were big wheels with cogs on them and grass growing inside them. Then, at the bottom of the shed, we could see another door that was new and looked very out of place amongst all the junk. We opened the door and peered inside; it was completely in darkness.

"You go first," said Doris who I could tell was scared.

I felt around for a light switch and eventually I clicked on the switch, it worked and a bright fluorescent light came on. There were two large workbenches with smooth surfaces, on one was what looked like a small press, on the other were brushes and cutters of all different shapes and sizes; there were also two boxes.

"Let's look in the boxes. You look in the one and I will look in the other" I said to Doris.

We opened the boxes together; Doris's box was packed with coloured crystals and mine was packed with jewellery resins.

"That's strange, what would Veronica need this equipment for, she's a beautician, not a jewellery maker. I didn't see any jewellery in the shop did you, Shirley?"

"No, I didn't but I bet this is where the forged jewellery came from. Quick, let's get out of here before Veronica realises what we have seen, she is obviously involved as well."

We ran out of the shed as fast as we could, making sure to leave everything the way we had found it. Then we calmly walked back into the salon just as Veronica was putting the final touches to Aunt Kate.

"Hi girls, what have you been up to? You were a long time; I hope you didn't go into the shed it is not safe," said Veronica.

"No, we did not go into the shed, we just sat on the grass." We both replied.

Both our faces had gone bright red and Veronica just stared at us as if she didn't believe us.

We all left and had a laugh with Aunt Kate, saying that she looked too young to be Evie's Mum, after her facial and makeover. In fact, the makeup had made her look even older but, of course, we didn't tell her that.

After that, Doris and I slowed our pace till we were out of earshot of the others, so we could discuss what we had just discovered.

"Now I know why she always gives me the creeps; she is as bad as Kevin and they are plotting together. I think we should tell somebody," said Doris pulling an awful face.

"Look Doris, we have no proof yet. We must wait for now and see what happens," I said reassuringly.

We carried on walking down the street and then Evie pointed to a posh looking jewellery shop.

"This is where I work," she said.

We all looked through the window. The window display was beautiful.

"These are Guernsey pearls. Aren't they lovely?" said Evie.

Around the pearls were really sparkly diamonds and objects of all descriptions.

"Let's go in, I will introduce you to Miss Blackly, she is the manager." continued Evie.

As we opened the door an old bloke in a black uniform came out.

"Hello Ben, this is my Mum, my cousin and her friend," said Evie.

Ben came right up close to us, "Hello, I am Ben and have been the security guard here for two years."

He seemed very nice but he was a bit old and short-sighted to be a security guard.

When we entered the shop, we could see an elderly lady behind the counter.

"This is Miss Blackly," said Evie.

Once the introductions were over with, Miss Blackly took us over to a small display cabinet in the middle of the shop.

"Come and see these, they are the most expensive items in the shop." remarked Miss Blackly as she led us to a small glass cabinet in the middle of the shop.

There was a pearl necklace that had one hundred Guernsey pearls and cost ten thousand pounds. There were rings and diamond necklaces that were priced at unbelievable prices.

Aunt Kate spotted some cuff links, "Your Dad would like those, Shirley," she said.

"Yes, I am sure he would, but he won't be getting them." I hastily replied. They were marked up at five thousand pounds. "Unless you want to buy them Aunt Kate," I joked. She just laughed.

Miss Blackly asked Evie. "What days are you working this week? I have a lot of paperwork for you to do."

"I am not in this week but will be in next week," replied Evie.

Miss Blackly looked very disappointed with Evie's answer. She looked the type that was highly efficient and would have liked Evie to do it right now.

"How did you get this job and what do you do? You know nothing about jewellery," asked Aunt Kate.

"I deal with the import and export licenses and sometimes I work behind the counter. Kevin organised it for me, to save me from getting bored. He knows the shop owner," Evie replied looking quite horrified that Aunt Kate had said such a thing, "And I do know something about jewellery, thank you."

Ben the security guard came back into the shop and nearly fell over Doris, who was fastening up her trainers.

"Sorry" said Doris and got up quickly grabbing Ben to stop him falling into the counter.

"That's OK, I do it all the time. The old eyes are not as good as they used to be". Ben muttered trying to balance himself at the same time.

"Come on, let's go before we cause any more accidents," said Evie.

We said Goodbye to everyone and left.

We were all exhausted and Evie phoned for a taxi. Doris and I were really glad. We didn't fancy the long walk back, carrying all the shopping.

When we arrived back Kevin was already at home, making the tea. It was a joint effort to carry all the shopping in, we dropped all the bags in the hall.

"Have you had a nice day?" asked Kevin who had popped his head around the kitchen archway. "Cool hats, girls!" he added, not able to hide his laughter.

"Yes, we have had a really nice day, thanks. We even went to that nice hotel, the one I have wanted to go to for a long time. You know the one I mean; the really posh one," said Evie.

"Why did you go there?" asked Kevin, his laughter suddenly gone. His voice was abrupt and, out of nowhere, there was a real sharpness and angry tone in his voice. "WHY? Did you go there?" he repeated.

"Why not there?" replied Evie looking quite surprised.

Kevin looked down to the floor. "Sorry, no reason. I just thought I would take you there one day" he muttered. "Anyway, come on we are going to have a real American tea. We are going to have gut buster burgers and fries followed by cherry pie and loads of Guernsey cream." His voice was back to normal now, but there was still a chilly atmosphere in the room.

The tea was wonderful, Doris and I managed three large burgers each and two helpings of cherry pie. We only ate burgers at home if it was a real treat or if we went to the seaside. Mum, who was always on some kind of diet, could not resist them and so we didn't get them either.

Doris kicked me under the table; this was usually the drill when she was going to ask something that was going to help us with our investigations. "Kevin could we please see your study? Evie said it was an old chapel and I would love to see it." she pleaded.

He looked up from the table

"Yes, of course, but you will have to give me ten minutes to tidy up and put away my documents. I will let you in when I am ready" he replied and off he went towards the study.

Doris and I followed him quietly; he picked up the briefcase that never left his side and proceeded to enter the code on the security door.

"Doris, try and see the code," I whispered.

She was doing well, she had crept right up behind him and then, suddenly, she gave out a loud sneeze! I just shook my head whilst Kevin covered the keypad with his hand, then he went into the study and closed the door behind him.

"Did you manage to see any of the numbers?" I asked.

"Yes Shirley, I did, the first number was definitely a three and then I sneezed so I didn't see any more".

Eventually, after a lot of shuffling and furniture moving Kevin opened the door and let us in. It looked very old almost medieval with fine stone archways and large pillars of marble. It was quite dark with nooks and crannies everywhere and at the back was an old altar that was draped in red velvet cloth. Doris was looking around and I thought I would question Kevin.

"Have you heard about the secret tunnel and the old monk's bible?" Kevin took a deep breath and stared at me.

"Yes, I have, but it's all nonsense; people in this country love a legend. Even better if it involves secret tunnels. You will be telling me next that the house is haunted by a monk's ghost or some evil spirit. It's all very whimsical," he replied.

I must admit what he said was probably true, but I did not want to disappoint Doris too much. This was her thing and it really excited her; better for her to learn herself.

Doris was looking under tables and in every little hiding hole, she could see into. "What's this?" She asked. She appeared to have some dusty old book in her hand and was showing us both as she was patting the dust off it.

"Ah, that is an old monk's bible and it was found hidden up in the chimney when the last owner of the house was redecorating. You can take it to look at if you want to, but most of it is unreadable," replied Kevin.

Doris, whom I could tell was really excited, said, "Oh yes please I will be very careful with it".

I was trying to look at the paperwork on the study desk, but Kevin had turned everything over to stop us from seeing.

"Come on now girls, out you get, I have work to do." He replied as he walked us towards the door and he let us out.

Doris was clutching the old dusty bible and I could tell she couldn't wait to start reading it.

Aunt Kate and Evie were sitting in the garden enjoying the last rays of the evening sun when we joined them.

"What a day we have had, I think tomorrow we will have a day at home and relax," said Evie.

"That seems like a good idea. What do you two think?" asked Aunt Kate.

We looked at each other and agreed.

"Yes, we still have lots of exploring to do," said Doris.

We all started talking about our shopping trip and Evie's jewellery shop.

"Evie, do you ever wear that beautiful necklace? The one I had to send here, by post!" asked Aunt Kate curiously.

"Yes, but only on special occasions or when Kevin is entertaining clients" Evie replied.

Now, I thought, this is our chance. "Evie, could we please see it again?" I asked.

"Yes, of course, when we go to bed, I will show it to you". Evie replied without hesitation."

Doris put on a fake yawn. It was a real loud one and her jaw was moving from side to side. "I am really tired; can we go to bed now?" Doris eventually managed to ask.

I didn't know whether the yawn was to see the necklace or so she could start reading her old book, but whatever, it worked.

Aunt Kate and Evie nodded and got up from their seats and walked into the house.

Evie headed for the study door, "We are all shattered, we are going up to bed," she shouted to Kevin. "How long will you be?"

"About an hour," Kevin replied. "Goodnight"

As we got to the top of the stairs, Evie pointed to her bedroom, "Come on, I will show you my necklace," she said and we all followed her.

Her bedroom was even bigger than Aunt Kate's. On the dressing table was a large wooden jewellery box with the "cute" teddy bear that we had got from Evie's house sat just in front of it. As she opened it, a little ballerina popped up and slowly spun around to some waltz music that played. Inside, I could see the ruby necklace which she handed to me carefully.

As soon as I held it, I knew that this was a different one; it was lighter. When I held it up to the light the red heart, which had been so clear and perfect, had scratches in it and the diamonds did not sparkle like the original one. Yes, I thought, this one is a forgery!

"It's lovely," I said and handed it back to Evie.

She laid it back in the box on top of what looked like an emerald bracelet.

"What's that?" asked Doris.

"Oh, it's another present from Kevin" Evie replied, smiling.

"Wow, you are a spoilt girl," said Aunt Kate.

Doris yawned again, this time I think it was genuine and I yawned too.

Once safely in our rooms where nobody could hear us, we both sat on our beds.

"Doris, did you see that emerald bracelet? I suspect that it's the one that was taken, with the necklace, from the jewellers in New York. Get the picture of the article on your phone Doris and let's recap on what it says," I instructed.

Doris searched on her phone and found it. There was no picture of the bracelet but I was convinced that it was the one.

Doris agreed "Just the Cartier cigarette box still to find!" she said.

I told Doris that I was convinced that the necklace had been swapped and it was not the one that Evie wore on her wedding day; it was a replica or a forgery. Doris went very quiet.

"What's wrong?" I asked. Doris took a deep breath.

"Don't get cross, Shirley, but what if Evie is in on it as well. If you think about it, there were two people in that jewellery shop. Maybe it could have been Evie. We know that they were both in New York at the same time. It could be possible".

I could feel my face getting hot. I was really annoyed, but I thought of Sherlock Holmes and did my best to put any sentiment aside. There could be a point here, I thought it through logically.

"Yes, Doris I see where you're coming from, but I know Evie and the only thing that she is guilty of is being used by Kevin and Veronica. And I, or we, will prove it. Now, no more doubting, get your notebook out and we will write down the facts," I said very calmly.

Doris found her notebook and pen, while I dictated what she was to write:

"Point 1: We know this jewellery is stolen from Madison Avenue New York.

"Point 2: The teddy bear was used to smuggle the jewellery through customs.

"Point 3: We know that replicas were used in the shop to fool shop assistants and I believe that the necklace we saw tonight was another replica.

"Point 4: Veronica has all the equipment safely tucked in her workshop to make the replicas and she did not want us going anywhere near it. That was suspicious.

"Point 5: Kevin was really cross about us going to that restaurant today. Why?

"Point 6: I am concerned about why Kevin found Evie a job in a jewellery shop.

"What we have to do now is get into Kevin's study and have a good rummage," I said. "Tomorrow I will think of a plan." Doris and I yawned again, "OK Doris, put that notebook away now and, remember, not a word to Aunt Kate," I said tiredly. "See you in the morning."

"Goodnight then" Doris replied.

Chapter 7 - The Riddle

The early night must have done us both good. Doris was already dressed and reading the old monk's bible when I woke up.

"Good morning Shirley, I have something to show you," said Doris.

"Are you OK Doris? Sounds exciting but before I do anything else I must phone Dad and Mum before they go to work. I promised them." I replied.

"Yes, that's fine I have already phoned mine and everything is fine," muttered Doris.

I picked up my phone and sat in the large chair by the window to call them. I eventually got through, Mum was excited; her new cooker was being delivered tomorrow and Dad was looking forward to a gourmet meal.

"Fingers crossed maybe no more burnt offerings for tea, but we will see, I will keep you informed," Dad laughed. They were both rushing off to work but it was lovely to hear from them.

I walked back to the bed and sat down. "Now then Doris, what have you got to show me?"

Doris sat up on the bed and showed me the bible. "I really don't know what language this is written in. It has a bit of French and then a bit of Latin I don't really understand any of it," she said, sounding puzzled.

"Is there any mention of a secret tunnel then?" I asked trying hard to look interested.

Doris went to the very last page. "Look, tucked in the back cover was this piece of paper, it was hidden in the spine of the book and I found a pair of tweezers and wiggled it out; it is some kind of riddle but it doesn't make much sense to me shall I read it to you?" said Doris.

I must confess I was a bit intrigued.

"Go on then, read it slowly to me" I replied.

We twelve monks are very poor,
No gold or silver in our store.
To speak of this, we are forbidden,
To survive, our secret must be hidden.
There is a painting on the wall,
Study that and you'll know all.
Behind the church by the crying tree,
A solitary face you'll see.
It stands alone both day and night,
Take its hands and hold on tight,
Six turns left and six turns right,
Then pull its arms with all your might.

"Is that it, Doris?" I asked.

"Yes, it seems to be. What a strange thing to find. What do you think it means Shirley?"

I thought about my answer for a minute. "Well, it seems to me that these monks were up to something that they shouldn't have been. And later on, we will follow clues and look at all the old paintings in the house, but remember Doris the painting may no longer be here and so don't be disappointed, but we will try."

"That sounds good" Doris replied. She sounded a little bit depressed about the painting no longer being there, but we had to be realistic. I knew she really wanted to find that secret tunnel.

"Now, back to solving crimes not mysteries Doris. We need a plan to get into Kevin's study so think, THINK!" I said, getting up and pacing back and forth, between our beds, deep in thought. "I know! We need to create a distraction, so that Kevin comes running out of his study, and then, we shall sneak in."

"Wow that sounds very scary to me," said Doris.

"I have a plan, get out the notebook Doris, and write this down:

"Aunt Kate and Evie will probably go for a walk this afternoon because it's a beautiful day. Doris, you can say you don't feel very well and if Kevin is here, we will pretend to be sunbathing in the garden. I will run in and say that you have fallen out of a tree you were climbing. He will come running out and as he leaves the study, I will wedge open the door. He will carry you into the kitchen; you can say you've really hurt your knee. I will insist on getting you a blanket from upstairs. Doris, you will have to make a real fuss and cry for about ten minutes. I will bring you the blanket having first checked that the study door is still wedged open. Then, I will feign shock and say I have to go upstairs and rest. I will get into the study, shut the door behind me and hide somewhere in there. You can then make a sudden recovery and say you are going upstairs to check on me, remember to limp a little, then you can tell Kevin from the top of the stairs that he can go back to work as we are both OK," I looked at Doris in anticipation, "Well, what do you think then?" I asked.

"It sounds a bit complicated, but I suppose it's worth a try. How are you going to get out of the study? Kevin can be in there for hours," asked Doris.

"Yes, I've thought of that. You know there is a house phone in the hall? You can ring that from your mobile, leave your mobile in the kitchen, answer the house phone and pretend that there is an urgent phone call for him. When he comes out, I will quickly follow and sneak out. I can hide in the cupboard under the stairs until he goes back into his study. But, remember Doris you must make the worst fuss about your knee. We will smear mud and red felt pen on your jeans. With you writhing around in pain he will think its blood, you are good at drama, aren't you?" I said.

"I am Shirley, but I shall be very nervous, what if it all goes wrong?" sighed Doris.

"Look, we have to get in there somehow and it's a flawless plan. Now, let's get some breakfast and we can start hunting for that painting in your riddle."

Doris was right, if things did not go to plan, we would be in so much trouble, but we had to try.

Chapter 8 - Art and star performances

We had our breakfasts and left Kevin, Aunt Kate and Evie in the kitchen and we went to check out all the paintings to see if we could solve the strange riddle. We started with the bedrooms, there were ten of them, but all the paintings on the wall seemed to be new. On the gallery there were paintings but none of them seemed to have any resemblance to what the riddle was saying. After about an hour we went downstairs and walked into the kitchen, there were no paintings in there.

"What are you two looking for?" asked Evie.

"We are just looking for really old pictures and paintings," I replied.

"Ah, all the old paintings are in the dining room and library; there was a lot of them in Kevin's study but we have moved them to the library," said Evie after thinking hard about her answer.

"Thanks" we both replied and ran into the dining room.

All the paintings in the dining room were of flowers and herbs, there was nothing with faces or any portraits. I looked at Doris; she was looking quite sad now.

"Come on Doris, let's look in the library, it's our last hope. We won't give up yet," I said, trying to cheer her up a bit.

In the library there was about twenty paintings on the walls.

"You start one side and I will start the other and we will meet in the middle," I said.

So we began, we studied every little detail on each painting, but nothing was making any sense; after about half an hour we met by the fireplace.

"This is the last one" Doris muttered.

It hung above the fireplace and we couldn't see it very well. Years of soot and smoke had made it really dark and dirty. We got two chairs and stood on them and used our mobiles to shine a light on it. The picture was of a monk standing in front of a small church ringing a bell and there was a large herb garden behind him. We stared and stared at it.

"Doris, read that riddle again," I said. Doris read it slowly. "What, I wonder, is a crying tree?"

We both stared at it again and then suddenly Doris shouted. "A weeping willow tree, look there, it is behind the church".

We shone our phones on it and tip toed higher on the chairs. Sure enough, there was a weeping willow tree, I could see Doris was really excited. She always shuffled her feet from side to side as if she had cramp or was dying to go to the toilet when she was nervous or excited. By the weeping willow tree in the background, we could just see a wooden block and I realised it was that strange looking sundial in the garden.

"It's that sundial; it has a face and hands, that's what the riddle must mean," I replied. "All that time we had been looking for human faces."

"Yes, of course Shirley and those funny bars on the sides must be what the riddle refers to as its 'arms'," Doris said, with a huge smile. "We have cracked the riddle! That's great."

Just then, Aunt Kate and Evie appeared in the doorway and we nearly jumped out of our skins we were so focused on the painting.

"Say nothing yet," I whispered to Doris.

"What on earth is all the excitement about? Be careful you both don't fall off your chairs," said Aunt Kate.

"Nothing really, we have just found the painting we have been looking for all morning" I replied.

Aunt Kate stepped forward and inspected the painting. "It's not very colourful is it, in fact it's very dull and boring. Why were you looking for it anyway?" She asked.

"It's just a riddle in a book, it has kept us busy all morning anyway" I replied.

"Well, its eleven o'clock now so we all have time for a walk before lunch, it is such a nice day. Are you two coming?" She continued.

I glared at Doris.

"Do you mind if I don't come, I am feeling a bit poorly; nothing much but a bit light headed," said Doris.

"Yes, that's fine. Kevin will be here until after lunch, but if I were you two, go and get a drink and sit quietly in the garden. The fresh air will do you both good. You've been in the house all morning," said Evie.

"That's a good idea, I will stay with Doris". I replied already thinking about our next move to get into that study.

Aunt Kate and Evie left for their walk and Doris and I went into the kitchen and took two glasses of water and a red felt tip pen into the garden.

"This is it now Doris, are you ready for full drama mode? Kevin is in his study. Now, let's find a suitable tree for you to fall out of," I said.

Doris looked very nervous. "I'm as ready as I can be, but I don't really have to fall from the tree, do I?" she asked.

"No, of course not, just stick to the plan Doris and don't panic. This beech tree here by the patio will do. Let's smear your jeans with this mud and water and add some red felt tip pen to look like blood," I studied her carefully, helping her to get into a convincing position. "That's perfect. Now, just lie on the floor and start acting. Look at your watch, remember to give me about twenty minutes in the study," she nodded at me with a nervous but determined look on her face. I smiled, reassuringly at her and we took a deep breath. "OK, Here goes!"

Everything after that seemed to happen really quickly. I ran to Kevin's study door and began hammering on it.

"There's been an accident, Doris has fallen out of a tree! Come quickly." I screamed at the top of my voice.

I was very impressed with my theatrical performance and, as planned, Kevin rushed out onto the patio. I placed an old paperback book in the study door to save it from closing and quickly followed Kevin. When I arrived in the garden, Doris, in all fairness, was giving it the performance of her life; she was writhing around crying and screaming. Our drama teacher would have been really proud of her. Kevin was quite cool about it, he picked her up and took her to the sofa in the kitchen.

"I'll go for a blanket," I said.

On the way back I checked that the door was still wedged open and returned to the kitchen. Doris was still crying and thrashing her legs around so that he couldn't see what actually had happened and what damage had been done. She could have won a BAFTA for that performance I thought to myself. Doris who was now getting tired stared at me to encourage me to hurry up with the next part of the plan. My turn now I thought.

"OH, OH Kevin, I really feel sick myself now. It must be shock I am going to lie down," I rushed out of the kitchen and went into the study making sure I closed the door behind me. I climbed under the alter and hid behind the red velvet curtain that was draped upon it. Just then I heard everything go quiet from the kitchen.

Doris had stopped her crying and wailing; "I feel better now, I must go and see if Shirley is OK upstairs," I heard her say.

"Are you sure? Should I phone the doctor?" said Kevin, panicking.

"No, I am fine now, thank you," insisted Doris and I heard her go upstairs.

I hoped she had remembered to limp a little, but it didn't matter that much now. I was in the study.

A couple of minutes later, I heard Doris shout down from the top of the stairs. "Shirley is well now Kevin; you can go back to your study."

So far so good. Kevin came back in the study and sat at his desk. I found a small gap in the curtain and peeped through it. Suddenly, I remembered to switch my phone off. Phew! That was lucky, I thought.

Kevin picked up his mobile phone and called somebody, "Hi, it's me. Sorry I am late but them noisy girls had some kind of accident. I will meet you at four o'clock at the usual place. We'd better not go to the hotel today; Evie took the family there yesterday it will look too suspicious. I will bring Evie's passport with me and we can discuss from there. See you later."

I wondered whom he was talking to.

Then, he moved the large wooden desk to one side, under it was a loose wooden floorboard that he lifted out. Hidden in it was a large tin that he placed on the desk and opened. Inside, I could just about see, was the ruby necklace the green emerald bracelet and a silver cigarette box.

That's where all the real jewellery is then. So, he was very guilty. It was not a mistake. Then to my shock and horror he pulled out another smaller tin, this contained more jewellery that I recognised, they were replicas of the jewellery we had seen in Evie's shop, that Miss Blackly had showed us. Guernsey pearl necklaces, cuff links and other pieces that we had seen in the shop. He placed this smaller tin in his briefcase; put the larger tin back under the floor boards and dragged the desk back to its original position. He took a passport out of the drawer and two large documents and then placed these on the desk. I couldn't see the writing very well, but I managed to read the larger letters on each document. One read 'Last Will and Testimony' and the other one read 'Business insurance'. He sat down at the desk and started reading them and making notes.

Who's will? I wondered, and who's business insurance?

The sound of the phone made me jump and then I heard Doris knocking on the door.

"Kevin, there is someone asking to speak to you on the hall phone" Doris said.

"Tell whoever it is, that I am too busy and that they will have to phone back," shouted Kevin.

Oh, that was not supposed to happen. How was I going to get out of here now?

Just before I got into a panic Doris knocked the door again.

Kevin stood up from his chair shaking his head and looking angry. "OK, OK I will come now," he muttered under his breath.

Thank goodness for that, but I would have to move fast. I ran to the door and made my escape. Unfortunately, I did not have time to see what else was on his desk. But I got through the door and climbed into the broom cupboard, falling into a metal bucket.

Of course, when Kevin picked up the phone there was nobody there.

I could hear him whining. "What a waste of my time, don't answer it again," he said and then he went back into his study and shut the door behind him.

I had trouble trying to untie myself from the broom cupboard and my foot had got caught in a bucket that had some water in it. Well, I hoped it was water anyway.

"Quick let's get upstairs I will tell you what I saw. We have got some more clues to put in our note book." I said to Doris. There were so many questions to answer: Why the passport? Why the replica jewellery? Who's business insurance? And, most importantly, who's will did he have in his desk? Doris and I wrote everything down but could not yet make any conclusions. The facts were obvious, he was up to something very wrong and, as yet, we could do nothing about it. Only watch and listen.

Doris who was looking quite concerned said, "Should we tell somebody Shirley, it could be very dangerous you know?"

"Look Doris, we must stay calm and keep our wits about us. Now, take a deep breath and everything will fall into place; you know, like it does in the books"

Doris just shrugged her shoulders and eventually she replied "OK".

Evie and Aunt Kate had come back from their walk unnoticed and were shouting that lunch was ready. We both ran downstairs. Kevin was telling Aunt Kate about the tree fall and about me being poorly.

"They look alright to me," said Aunt Kate and we all sat down for a quick lunch.

"Evie, have you got any plans for later? I was thinking of inviting a few clients around for dinner tonight, is that a problem?" asked Kevin.

"It's a bit short notice, but if I keep it simple and Mum helps me… I can manage that," replied Evie.

"Good, there will be eight of us and you can all wear the new clothes you bought the other day. They are all very important clients. I will invite Veronica to make up the numbers." continued Kevin, getting up from the table. "We will dine at half past eight that will give you plenty of time. I have got to go out now. I will see you all later," He picked up his briefcase and left.

Aunt Kate and Evie love cooking, and so, out came the cookery books and two aprons.

"It's a long time since we have cooked together, I am really going to enjoy this. Now, do you two girls want to come to the dinner party or would you rather have your tea earlier?" asked Aunt Kate.

I looked at Doris. "The dinner party sounds exciting we will come to that. It will be a good excuse to put on our party dresses that our Mum's insisted on packing," we both replied.

Aunt Kate nodded. "That's fine, but remember to behave yourselves; no being stupid or giggling!"

"As if!" I replied.

Chapter 9 - Doris's Excitement

Doris was still excited about solving the riddle. She suggested we left Evie and Aunt Kate busy in the kitchen and we could head out to the garden or maybe go for a walk. I had forgotten all about it, because, really, I thought the whole thing was just a ridiculous waste of brain space. But, little did I know...

"We're going for a walk," I said.

"Don't go out of the gates at the bottom of the drive" shouted Aunt Kate.

She had to shout for us to hear above the sound of food mixers and other kitchen gadgets. I noticed Doris shuffle over to the cooker and put something in her pocket, but I couldn't see what exactly it was.

We ran to the garden and Doris ran straight to the sundial and we both stared at it.

"What do we do now Shirley?" asked Doris.

I knew I had to show myself to be interested otherwise Doris would get into a sulk.

"Let's see, let's get one each side of it and hold onto these bars (arms in the riddle), then we can turn these pointers (hands in the riddle), six turns left and then six turns right and pull. It looks a bit rusty to me though." I answered.

We followed the instructions and pulled and tugged. But nothing seemed to be happening.

After several attempts and a lot of huffing and puffing Doris, who was very red in the face, said, "There must be a starting point, maybe we should put the pointers to twelve o'clock; after all, twelve is the only number mentioned in the riddle".

I really did not see what a difference that would make and by now I was getting well fed up of all this pulling.

Doris could tell, "Look Shirley I will do this by myself if you like. You can go back in the kitchen and make a fairy cake or something!"

"Calm down Doris, we will have one last attempt to make you happy". I said sarcastically.

Doris turned both pointers to twelve o'clock and we began the process again. "Hold on tight and pull Doris" suddenly there was a strange rumbling sound coming from underground. "Keep pulling," I said.

Slowly the wooden block of wood started to come apart. We pulled and pulled and eventually it revealed a hole just big enough for a person to squeeze through. We both stood and looked into the hole in amazement. We could see that were steps leading down the hole.

"We need some kind of light," I said. Doris went into her pocket and pulled out a large box of matches.

"See Shirley, you're not the only one who thinks logically! I knew we would find the tunnel, so I took these from the kitchen earlier," she replied, looking really smug.

"Well done, Doris, now strike a match and you go first. After all, you have found the tunnel," I said.

That seemed to please her and so she squeezed herself onto the first step and struck the match; down we went onto the second step and third step lighting matches as we were going. We stopped and both noticed a strange smell.

"What's that smell?" asked Doris.

"I've smelt it before," I said, frowning, trying to place the memory. "For some reason, it reminds me of Christmas."

Eventually we reached the bottom step, we were in a large cave. All around the walls were candles in wall-mounted holders.

"Give me the matches Doris, let's light these old candles on the wall and then we will be able to see better."

They took some lighting but eventually we managed to light some of them. Once our eyes had focused, we could see what was around us.

There were big copper containers everywhere, about ten of them. There were barrels and bottles everywhere and, in the middle, was what looked like a small railway track with a little sledge on it. We walked over to one of the barrels. It was empty, but when we looked inside, we could smell that strange smell again. It smelt like some kind of drink. Maybe brandy, I thought.

"My Dad drinks something that smells like this at Christmas. These monks must have been secretly distilling alcohol. The track must have been used for carrying it to different places to sell. Probably down to the coast. Let's walk down the track and see where it goes to?" suggested Doris.

"Yes, but be careful you have already fallen out of a tree today" I replied, knowing there was no stopping her now.

"Very funny ha-ha," Doris replied.

As we walked down the track, we lit the candles that lined the walls. It was slow progress but, eventually, after about five minutes, we came to a junction in the tunnel. The one tunnel turned down a steep slope the other tunnel went sideways to the left

"Which way shall we go?" asked Doris.

We decided to carry on down the slope. It seemed to get very steep and we held onto each other. There were cobwebs and insects everywhere, but we kept going until all we could see was a large rock blocking our way.

"Oh dear, looks like the end of the line" I said. Doris who was not giving up was crawling on the floor.

"Look Shirley, I can see daylight and this hole at the side of the rock is just big enough for us to crawl through," she said.

"I will go first I am bigger than you and if I get stuck you will have to run back and get help" I muttered.

"Yes, I am slimmer than you," she replied.

I got down on my hands and knees and pushed my way through the small hole; it took some twisting and turning but eventually I made it. Doris was close behind and we emerged into the daylight. Our eyes had become adjusted to the darkness of the tunnel, but soon we could see that we were on the beach. It was a small beach cove and the sea was just in front of us. The tide was going out which I thought was very fortunate otherwise how would we be able to get back home? There was nobody about and the beach was very secluded.

"The monks must have brought their barrels down here on the sledge and track and then they would have met ships and boats to transport their goods. They must have been smugglers and in those days, it would have been very illegal. Especially for monks to be doing it. If they had been caught, they would have been executed or thrown in jail. No wonder they kept it a secret," Doris said.

"We should have got on the sledge it would have been quicker," I said. Just then, we could hear some voices around the corner. "Quick Doris, hide behind these rocks we do not want anybody else discovering our tunnel yet."

We hid behind the small rocks and waited quietly; the voices were coming nearer. Two people came into view and sat down, just in front of the rocks. We both looked at each other, eyes wide and gasped quietly.

It was Kevin and Evie. How could that be? We had left Evie busy in the kitchen with Aunt Kate.

Kevin had his arm around Evie and they were chatting. I signalled to Doris and we moved to a closer rock. Evie's red hair was shining in the sun and it hung over her shoulders like it always did. She was wearing that blue striped shirt that she had bought on our shopping trip. She turned for a second to look behind her. I hoped she hadn't heard us; that would take some explaining.

Doris and I must have realised at exactly the same time, because we both put our hand to our mouths in astonishment. It was Kevin, but it wasn't Evie, it was Veronica! She was wearing some of Evie's clothes and a red wig. What on earth was all this about? We calmed down and listened to their conversation. Kevin was holding Veronica's hand.

"Look Kevin, I do not like those meddling girls, they are up to something. I do not trust them. I think we should go ahead with the job now and not wait any longer. Did you bring Evie's passport? I will go into her bank tomorrow and transfer all the funds to our American account. You could do it but it looks less suspicious if they think Evie is doing it. I think by the time the police work everything out we will be long gone." Kevin handed over the passport.

"I have checked that Fairbank's business insurance is up to date. We will see him tonight to discuss arrangements. Do you have all the replicas done? And is your speedboat all ready? We can plan our departure later at the dinner party. We can no longer use the hotel in town as our meeting place; Evie went there with the family. Anyway, it will be obvious to the police that Evie has committed the crime. It's the right time to do the job, I agree," Kevin said, smiling and looking really evil. They got up and began to walk off together, "I will see you later." We heard him say as they parted ways.

Doris and I were shocked, not only were they going to take all of Evie's money they were going to blame her for some dreadful crime.

"I wonder what crime it will be?" asked Doris.

"I don't really know, but I bet it's something to do with the jewellery shop that Evie works at. Who is Fairbanks? We need to find out tonight." I sadly replied.

Doris had that really worried look on her face, "How could they be so horrid to Evie, she is such a lovely person. And I don't believe Veronica is Kevin's sister either do you? What on earth are we going to do Shirley? This is very serious; we should tell Aunt Kate! We are definitely out of our depth here. It is all very well, you thinking like Sherlock Holmes, but this is no book," said a frightened Doris.

"Wow, so many questions Doris. Let's just think. Let's walk back up the tunnel and we can decide when we get back." I said, trying very hard to stay calm.

We crawled back through the hole in the gap in the rock; this time the tunnel seemed to be darker and damper and very muddy underfoot. We had used up all the matches and continued using the lights on our mobiles, but we knew there was not a lot of battery left in either of our phones. We would just have to hope we had enough to get us back.

Walking uphill was a lot harder and the black, thick cobwebs were determined to go in our faces and hair. What had started out as very exciting, had turned into a horrible situation.

Eventually we reached the junction point, were the rails split into two directions.

"Are we going to see where the other tunnel goes?" asked Doris.

"No, let's leave that until tomorrow, our phones need charging and I'm hot and just need to get out of here" I replied.

Doris didn't argue and so we climbed the steps and were both glad to breathe in the fresh garden air. We shut up the tunnel by pushing its arms together and it shut tight.

"I hope we will be able to open it again," said Doris as we rushed into the house. Evie and Aunt Kate were still in the kitchen and all the cooking had been done.

"Are you both all right? That was a very long walk, your shoes are very muddy and you look really hot," said Evie, staring at us. "Now, do you both want a snack, to keep you going until dinner?"

"No thank you Evie, we are exhausted and are going to have a rest before the party. We will see you later." I replied and we both ran up the stairs.

Aunt Kate shouted after us, "Remember to look smart and behave yourselves."

"Yes, we will," we both replied.

We both sat on my bed and Doris got the notebook out. "Do you want to hear what I think?" said Doris.

"Yes of course I do, but it doesn't mean I will agree" I replied.

Doris continued. "Let's take it one step at a time. First, we have got to stop them from transferring Evie's money; there must be a way of doing that. It is obvious that Veronica is pretending to be Evie, in her clothes and that ridiculous wig. It's no wonder people in the town are saying strange things to Evie. Remember Shirley, when we went into that restaurant and the waiter asked her if she wanted her usual table."

"Yes, of course Doris, you're right, she does have a double, it's Veronica. Now, I have worked out a plan; the bank will not transfer the money without a valid passport so we need to phone up the passport office and cancel it. We can pretend that Evie has lost it."

"That's a good idea, but we would have to tell Evie. They would not cancel it for anybody else and they will ask her security questions," replied Doris.

"I have thought of that. You will have to pretend to be her on the phone" I said cautiously, knowing Doris would object.

"Why is it always me?" Doris said, with a raised voice and her arms flapping around in protest.

"Well, because you sound older than me on the phone. Please Doris, it's very important." I pleaded with her. "Your telephone manner is brilliant and mine is not as good as yours, is it?"

Doris sighed and nodded. We looked up the telephone number for the passport office on our phones.

We followed the plan and eventually Evie's passport was stopped.

We both agreed that we felt a lot happier now we had done that. Time was ticking on and we decided to get ready for the party.

"Now, tonight Doris, we must listen to every conversation. Maybe we can get a clearer picture of what is going on and plan our next move." I said with anticipation and, maybe, a bit of dread.

Chapter 10 - And now we know

At eight o'clock, all dressed and both looking glamorous, we headed down the stairs. People were starting to arrive and everybody was mingling. Evie and Aunt Kate came over to us and told us how smart we looked. To be honest, Doris and I were wearing our Christmas party dresses, but nobody knew that.

Evie started introducing us to the guests. "This is Mr and Mrs Hardy, they live just up the road and this is Mr Fairbanks, he is my new boss who owns the jewellery shop that I work in."

I nudged Doris and whispered "Ah, so this is Fairbanks then."

"Yes, he looks a bit shifty," replied Doris and we both grabbed a glass of orange juice from a silver tray that was on the side table in the hall.

After saying 'Hello' to everybody, we eventually sat down in the dining room and got ready to eat.

"Use your napkins girls," said Aunt Kate.

How embarrassing I thought, but we just agreed quietly and Doris who could see I was embarrassed started to giggle. I kicked her under the table and we just sat there waiting for our food. Veronica, who was sitting opposite, was talking and laughing really loudly. The more I heard her, the more I disliked her.

Everybody was chatting and the conversation came around to America and holidays.

Feeling quite grown up and in charge of myself and trying to prove to Aunt Kate that I was not a child, I looked at Veronica straight in the eye and inquired. "Have you ever been to New York?"

She lifted her face up from her dinner and her eyes just glared at me.

I was feeling brave and just stared back at her.

"Of course, I have. That's a very stupid question to ask an American. All Americans have," she replied. There was a real gripe in her voice.

"No that's not a stupid question at all Veronica, I had a friend for many years who lived in Philadelphia, but she had never been to New York," remarked Aunt Kate as she smiled at me.

Veronica looked at Kevin and he nodded back to her. I think he thought then, that we knew too much and the conversation was changed quickly. Veronica went red and just shrugged her shoulders.

After dinner we all went to sit in the library and some wandered out on to the patio to smoke.

"Right Doris, we must trail Veronica and Kevin, we must also keep an eye open for Fairbanks. Are you up for it? We might have to split up, but we shall see." I whispered very quietly.

Kevin had been talking to Mr and Mrs Hardy about stocks and shares, but he looked really bored. He made some excuse and then headed straight for Veronica, out of his pocket he pulled out the Cartier cigarette case, well, that is what we presumed it must be as every other item that was stolen was in his possession. He flashed it about and started handing out little business cards.

"What a show off," said Doris.

I had to agree.

We watched as Veronica and Kevin slipped outside, unnoticed by the guests and headed to a secluded spot in the garden.

"Quick Doris," I whispered, following them and pulling her along with me. "We need to hear what they are saying."

We crept in some bushes just behind them and listened:

"Have you spoken to Fairbanks yet?" Veronica asked. "I have a plan; we can do the job next Tuesday night. I will figure a way to get your dreadful family out of the way. Then, on Friday, we can get the boat ready on the beach and I will arrange to meet the dealer in France on Friday evening. Make sure Fairbanks takes a holiday and you can tell that wife of yours that you are going on a business trip on the Friday. Fairbanks returns on Monday and discovers the crime. Evie will get arrested; by the time they realise that she is possibly innocent, we will be miles away in a different country with all of Evie's money and all of the money from the deal."

"Sounds perfect, I think you could be right about them meddling girls, I am very fed up with them and their stunts," said Kevin, sounding irritated. "I will speak to Fairbanks now."

Veronica walked away. Kevin went back to pour himself another drink and then walked across to Mr Fairbanks.

What a cruel calculated person he was. However, Veronica was going to be in for a shock tomorrow when she tried to transfer all of Evie's money. Doris and I had seen a bank statement on the kitchen table. We'd seen that there was five hundred thousand pounds in her account! And they planned to leave her with nothing.

Kevin managed to get Fairbanks on his own, but there was nowhere for us to hide, only a small garden table.

"I'll get under it shall I then?" said Doris, rolling her eyes.

Some of the other guests must have spotted her and wondered what she was doing, but that didn't stop her. She was very determined by then and we were desperate to find out exactly what was going on; just as long as Kevin didn't see her.

I watched from a distance, hoping that Doris was getting some useful information. Not able to keep still, I kept my eyes on them and started pacing. Not knowing what was being said was quite insufferable!

Finally, Kevin and Mr Fairbanks got up and parted ways. Doris crept from under the small table and adjusted her dress that was sticking out everywhere.

"Well Done, Doris, what did you hear?" I asked, impatiently.

Doris did not disappoint. She recalled the whole conversation back to me in precise detail:

"Well first, Kevin said, 'Right Fairbanks, listen very carefully. We are going to do the job on Tuesday night. You will have to make sure you're far away somewhere and get yourself an alibi, make sure loads of people know who you are. Then, on the Monday, you can return to the shop and discover that the original jewellery has been replaced with replicas. Listen, I have checked your insurance papers and you will be able to claim three times as much as the jewellery is worth. Just stay calm, follow the plan and keep your mouth shut then there will be no trouble. We have done it many times before. Are you up for it then? Remember tonight you have to make a big issue of giving Evie the keys and the alarm code so that there are plenty of witnesses.'

"So Fairbanks replied, 'OK, I will do it. I need that money; sales have been pretty slow lately. But if you double cross me I will track you and Veronica down and tell everybody.'

"And then Kevin said 'Just do as I have told you and everything will be fine,'" Doris finished with a grim look. "Then they both went back inside."

Unbelievable, I thought. Now I knew what the business insurance was for and exactly what they were up to. We had to stop them, but HOW? And the other question was, whose 'Last Will and Testimony' was Kevin so very interested in? This was very worrying.

A little later on, all of the guests were sitting on the patio drinking coffee to finish off the evening. Mr Fairbanks stood up and walked up to Evie.

"Now Evie, I am going away next week and I want you to have these," he said very loudly, so that everyone could hear him, out of his pocket he pulled two small keys and a piece of paper. He continued, "Miss Blackly has keys but I want you to have this security code. Ben has got the other half of this code. I really trust you, Evie. Please keep it safe."

"Oh, thank you for putting that trust in me. I will keep it really safe." Evie replied. She looked really pleased and Aunt Kate touched her on the hand, giving her approval, showing she was very proud of her. Doris and I just shook our heads. If only she knew what was going on.

Everybody was leaving and we headed for bed. We had so much to talk about; the secret tunnel, the monks and, most importantly, the plot to frame Evie.

Finally, discussions done and exhausted from the day's revelations, we soon fell to sleep.

Chapter 11 - The tunnel, take two

We woke up quite early; the house was really quiet, no one else had woken up yet. We went downstairs, made our way to the kitchen and got ourselves some cereal and fruit juice. Evie was taking Doris and I to some museums today and to see a little church that was covered with seashells. Doris was really looking forward to our day, I was not so keen, but at this point there was nothing we could do but just wait and the weekend was fast approaching, so it would give us time to think.

Everybody came down and, after they all had breakfast, we got ready and set off. Aunt Kate had decided to have a lazy day and we left her with a pile of books on the patio. Kevin was dropped off at his office; he was really quiet and didn't speak to us at all. We didn't care and were glad when he got out of the car.

The first place we went to was an underground German hospital. The tunnels were really long and very damp and stuffy, so we did not stay in them long, but they were really interesting. The poor prisoners of war that built them must have worked so hard and the guide that took us around was really good. She explained how many had died building the tunnels. They had been very brave. Doris absorbed every word and small detail that the guide explained to us. I was glad because we both needed some distraction from the upcoming crime.

The next place we visited was the small church covered with shells, it was beautiful. Evie had brought a picnic with us and we decided to eat it on the beach. We stretched our blanket out and sat looking over the sea.

"I love the sea, it's so wild and mysterious," said Doris.

We both agreed.

"Evie, have you sailed around the bay and the coastline of Guernsey?" I asked

"Yes, I have, Veronica has a speedboat and one afternoon we went sailing it was great, it's a lovely boat. She keeps it moored just around the corner, let's go and I will show you," replied Evie.

We grabbed our stuff and got back in the car. This was the answer I was hoping for because then we would know where Veronica's boat was kept. This could be of great importance later on.

We passed large German bunkers and some gun emplacements as we drove up onto a small car park. In front of us was a large tower.

"That's called Pleinmont bunker and just below is where Veronica moors her boat. She calls the boat 'The Crooked Lady'," said Evie, gesturing to a marina just visible at the bottom of the hill. "Right, we will head back to Castle Cornet now and go in the museum."

Doris and I smiled about the boat's name. How appropriate, we both thought.

When we arrived at the castle it was closed and so we decided to head back home. Evie thought that we had better check on Aunt Kate. There was no need to worry, when we got back, she was reading a book in the garden.

"Did you all have a good time?" Aunt Kate asked. "The peace has been lovely," she said, smiling at us. "It's time for a cup of tea," she decided. She put down her book and made her way to the kitchen.

"We will stay in the garden," Doris and I replied. We sat on the patio, talking about everything we had seen.

"I wonder if Veronica has been to the bank yet? I hope she failed," Doris said.

"Who knows, but I am sure we will hear something later. We must keep our wits about us." I replied, also desperately hoping that she had failed.

Doris took a deep breath, "I have been thinking, Shirley, we really should tell somebody," she muttered.

"You're always dangerous when you have been thinking. Look, let's wait until Saturday and then we can decide," I replied.

Doris did not look happy with my reply and I could see her lips tighten up and that worried look coming over her face. I knew I had to do something to distract her and cheer her up in case she gave the game away.

"Come on Doris, let's go and explore the monk's tunnel again and see where the other one goes. I will tell Aunt Kate and Evie we are going for a walk. What do you think?"

Her face lit up with excitement "Oh yes! Let's do that. I will go and fetch the matches, we have both charged our phones so we will be able to see better this time," replied a much happier Doris.

We got ourselves organised and prepared to enter the tunnel for the second time. Doris was looking much happier now, but underneath I knew she was right. Soon, we would have to tell somebody, but WHO?

We set off to the sundial and went through the motions of opening it. I was secretly hoping that it would open and that we hadn't shut it too tightly the last time. Luck was with us, it opened really easily and down the steps we went. Making sure we left a slight gap in case it got stuck. We lit the candles on the wall again, until we arrived at the junction.

"Let's get in the cart and go down slowly, it will save us the walk," said Doris.

"That sounds a good idea but let's go slow, we had better check that these brakes work," I said, eyeing the cart carefully. "What about lighting the candles? We cannot be in and out, so we will have to go in the dark," I said.

"I will keep lighting matches. There is plenty of them; I got a new box from the kitchen this morning. And, we can leave our torches on our phones on," replied Doris.

I remember thinking that Aunt Kate would not be happy because we knew that matches could be very dangerous.

We both sat in the cart, Doris was in the front holding the phones and matches and I sat at the back holding on to the brake lever, which was very stiff. The cart started to move, slowly at first and then, suddenly, it got faster and faster as if it was going down a steep hill. I was tugging on to the brake lever, seemingly to no avail, until it finally came to a halt after about two minutes.

We got out of the cart and decided to rest a bit and light some of the candles on the wall before we carried on.

It had been very scary travelling at speed in the dark and reminded me of a fairground ride I had been on with Dad whilst we were on holiday somewhere.

Looking around, we could see drawings on the wall and tally markings that must have been used for counting how many bottles of spirit they were selling.

Just below one of the candles was a large bell scraped into the wall with some writing inside it.

"Bring the phones over here Doris and shine the lights on this writing. It looks like another riddle," I said.

I was right and we read the riddle together:

"Us twelve monks had no time to pray
We had to work, the bills to pay
We brewed all day to make a living
The olde church fund was never very giving
Some of us lived double lives
Some of us even took a wife
The liquor we brewed was sold in town
We hid our money from the crown
Not one penny given for their taxes
If they'd found out, our heads would be under axes
We all agreed that on this day, to board a ship and
sail away
So, our parting gift for you to sell
Its hidden deep below this bell
Sell it wisely; give to the poor and needy
Or just like us you will become greedy"

"Doris let's take a picture and we can study it later. Let's get back in the cart and carry on exploring this tunnel".

Doris took a photo of it and we both got back in position and pushed the cart to start it off again. The cart began to move slowly and then it picked up speed

"Hold on Doris" I said. We were travelling at a very fast pace and the air was getting colder and colder and it was very dark. Suddenly the cart came to a sudden stop, hitting something solid and throwing us both out of the cart.

"Doris?" I screamed, "Are you ok?"

"I am fine. Just dusty and covered in cobwebs," Doris replied.

We got ourselves up and lit a match; we had hit a big wooden door. We found our phones and both shone the light on the door. There was a key in the keyhole and, eventually, we managed to open the door. We walked through into a small room. From above us we could hear laughing and talking.

"We are in somebody's cellar" whispered Doris.

There were stone archways and some stairs. We climbed up the stairs and slowly pushed open the door and we both peered through. It was a pub. We could see the customers and the barman, behind the bar, pouring drinks. We quickly shut the door and went back down the steps quietly. On the other side of the small room, was a small set of steps with a shutter at the top.

"Come on Doris let's see where these steps go to," I said with excitement.

At the top we pushed open the shutter and could see we were in the pub car park. There was nobody about and so we climbed out and closed the shutter behind us. We walked around to the front of the pub, it was on the Main Street and the pub was called 'The Monks Head'. It looked very old and had tiny windows and black and white timber everywhere.

"This must have been where the monks sold their goods! How clever of them to use the old tunnel," I said.

We looked around; just opposite was the jewellery shop were Evie worked. How handy was this going to be on Tuesday night, I thought, when Kevin and Veronica were going to commit their crime. We could sneak down the tunnel and see what was happening.

Doris, who knows me very well, said, "Don't go having any ideas, Shirley."

"Of course not, Doris. As if!" I deviously replied. "We had better get back."

We walked around the back of the pub, but as we walked, I secretly timed how many minutes it took us to get back down the steps and out of sight. It took exactly three minutes, and, if we had been running, we could do it even faster. Doris caught me looking at my phone and I am sure she knew what I was up to.

Once back in the pub we could see the wooden door was very well concealed behind wooden panelling, that's why nobody had ever spotted it. We pulled the panelling back over the wooden door and squeezed back into the tunnel. This time, we had to walk back up the tunnel and pull the cart with us, which was very heavy.

"Why can't we leave the cart where it is?" asked Doris.

"Well, we might need it on Tuesday night to make a quick trip to the jewellers," I quietly replied.

Even though it was very dark, I could feel Doris's eyes staring at me with dismay.

"I don't like the sound of that, Shirley. You always think you know best don't you. I think it could be very dangerous," she shouted.

I knew she was probably right.

"Don't worry, I know what I am doing. Now, let's get back and then we can study that second riddle left by the monks. I think we will have to find a shovel for some treasure hunting, but that will have to wait until another day". I uttered. That thought was quite intriguing I wondered what the monks had buried. It would probably turn out to be nothing, but we would see.

At last, we reached the tunnel entrance and we were exhausted. The cart that seemed to travel so fast downhill was really heavy to pull back up, but we had done it. Huffing and puffing and very red in the face we arrived at the entrance and climbed the stone steps out onto the garden.

We took a breath for a minute and then walked into the house through the patio door.

As we walked in, we could hear a mobile phone ringing and we ran into the hall. Kevin had just arrived through the front door. He had a small brown paper bag in his hand and was struggling to get his phone out of his pocket.

Eventually, he managed to answer the phone and he placed the brown paper bag on the hall table whilst he tried to cradle the phone between his ear and neck.

He looked aggravated and we could hear him saying, "Calm down, what exactly happened? Did they take the passport off you?" From the corner of his eye, he spotted us and knew we were listening. He waved his hand and tried hard to smile at us and then hurriedly entered his study shutting the door behind him, trying to continue his conversation on the phone.

"That must have been Veronica, she'll have been to the bank, they must have questioned her. That will teach her," I said and we both had a really good laugh about it.

Doris moved to the hall table and sitting on it was the small brown paper bag that Kevin, in his panic, had forgotten.

"What's in here then?" said Doris and we both peered in it.

"Let's look quickly," I said; It was a small blue bottle with POISON written on it. On the back were tiny pictures of what looked like insects.

"What is that for?" asked Doris.

"I don't know." I said in a panic, "But I really don't like it, it is sending shivers down my spine." I looked at Doris, "We have to do something," I said, thinking hard, "Right, run into the kitchen, pour it down the sink and I will look for something to replace it with in the cupboard,"

All we found was peppermint essence.

"That will have to do." We poured it into the bottle, replaced the cap and rushed to put it back in the bag on the hall table.

Kevin came out of the study looking really annoyed. "What are you two doing?" he said, in a harsh voice. "Why are you hovering there I am not in the mood for any of your silliness. Go and play somewhere else please," he continued. His true colours were starting to show now and he grabbed the paper bag off the table and went back into the study.

Doris and I thought how funny he was when he was in a bad mood, but we could not help thinking about what had just happened with the poison.

"Do you think he was going to poison us all?" asked Doris.

"No, of course not" I said, but I did wonder, it was obviously not going to be Evie as they wanted her to take the blame, but I did not really know about the rest of us!

Chapter 12 - Afternoon tea

Saturday arrived; we couldn't believe we had been here for a week already. We had found out loads of stuff about the pending crime and, of course, Doris had solved the mystery of the vanishing monks and their tunnel; we still had the treasure to dig up. Even though it was a joint effort, I thought that Doris should probably take most of the credit for it. In all fairness, I would not have had the patience to carry on looking. I was more concerned about the Kevin and Evie affair.

We still did not know exactly what was going to happen on Tuesday night, we still did not know who's will Kevin was so interested in and, of course, there was that bottle of poison.

I knew what a will was as I had seen one when an aunt of Mum's had died. Aunt Kate had brought it round to our house for close inspection. Of course, I had a good look at it and knew that it was the final wishes after someone had died and that it was a legal document.

It was pouring with rain and the wind was really blowing hard. Aunt Kate had forbidden us to go out as it was too dangerous and so we sat in the kitchen playing board games. In fact, it really was great fun.

Kevin got back at about three o'clock in the afternoon, he seemed in a better mood than yesterday. He had bought some cake and was busy telling Aunt Kate that it was a Guernsey specialty. Doris and I decided that it just looked like fruit loaf and nothing very special.

Evie stood up "I will put the kettle on, we can have tea with our cake," she said.

Kevin walked in front of her, blocking her route to the kettle, "No sit down, I will do it," he looked over at Doris and me, "Do you girls want lemonade?" he asked.

"Yes please" we both replied.

After a lot of fussing and fiddling, he brought over the drinks.

"Here is yours, mother-in-law" he said and placed it down in front of Aunt Kate.

The rest of the drinks were brought on a tray. The cake was sliced and we all had a piece. Aunt Kate picked up her tea and sipped it, I noticed her pull a strange face, but she didn't say anything. In fact, she went very quiet and picked up her cake. It really was very nice. But, then, Doris and I realised that Kevin did not have any cake.

"That was so nice I might need another piece, and this time you must have some Kevin," said Aunt Kate.

Kevin cut himself a piece, Doris and I waited until he had eaten his before we ate anymore and second helpings were brought around.

I looked at Doris, how silly and unprofessional had we been. The word cake had made us forget about the 'POISON'. Panic over, we tucked in again.

Aunt Kate sipped her tea again and, because it had cooled down, she must have taken a bigger gulp. This time she started coughing and spat it out all over the table, but she was still choking and her face went a strange colour. Evie rushed over and patted her on the back.

Eventually, Aunt Kate said, "I am so sorry, but it tastes horrid. It is like really intense peppermint."

Doris and I just gasped; Kevin was trying to poison Aunt Kate in front of us all!

Evie smelt the tea. "Oh Kevin, you have given Mum my peppermint tea that I drink when I am on my diet." She patted Aunt Kate gently on the back, "Are you all right Mum? It's a bit strong, but it won't hurt you," she explained.

Kevin was apologising and making Aunt Kate another cup of tea whilst Doris and I were trying to compose ourselves, we had nearly fallen off our chairs.

"Just goes to show how we can jump to the wrong conclusions, doesn't it, Shirley," said Doris very quietly.

"Well yes, but we are not usually wrong, anyway, good job we were. I don't know how we would have explained that one to Mum, with a dead Aunt Kate." Things started to settle down and Aunt Kate drank her proper cup of tea.

"I have booked a restaurant for Sunday lunch tomorrow, save us all bothering with cooking," Kevin announced. "You can all dress up because it's a very expensive restaurant. Evie, you can wear your ruby necklace and your emerald bracelet," He smiled at her apologetically and spoke directly to her, "Now Evie, I am very sorry but on Friday I have to go on a business trip abroad. Unfortunately, I cannot get out of it, even though I do not want to leave you," he continued, taking her hands in his gently.

Doris and I could not believe how cool and caring he pretended to be and we both felt really sick.

"That's fine," Evie said, smiling back at him, totally taken in. "I have plenty to do. I can go into work, because Mr Fairbanks is going on holiday somewhere so I can help Miss Blackly."

The doorbell rang and in walked Veronica with her usual smug face and annoying, loud voice "Hi there everyone, how's it all going?" she said.

"We are all fine, thank you. What brings you here?" asked Evie.

She did not need a reason, as she seemed to pop in and out as she pleased, but on this occasion, she had one. "I have had some tickets to a local operatic performance on Tuesday night from a client, I certainly do not want to go and listen to that noise." she said, making a face. "I wondered if you and Kate would like them? It's an opera called 'Carmen', but the tickets are in the name of Mrs and Miss Smith, you would have to pretend to be them. The performance starts at seven o'clock what do you think?" asked Veronica.

I could see Kevin was looking tense and looked at Veronica. "What a great idea! I will make sure I am in, I will get a movie and some popcorn for the girls to watch whilst you away," he remarked, looking very excitable.

I looked at Doris and wondered what they were up to. This was a good way to get rid of Aunt Kate and Evie for the night but what, exactly, were they plotting?

"Yes, thank you Veronica. We would love to go, wouldn't we Mum?" replied Evie who was looking at a nodding Aunt Kate.

Veronica gave Kevin a smug smile. "That's good, all settled then, bye for now then," she uttered. Then she left the room.

"I am going to do some work now," said Kevin and he followed her out.

I could hear the two of them chatting and laughing in the hall. I quietly got up from the table and went to listen, hiding behind an archway.

"That's got them out of the way. I will get to the shop at quarter passed seven and smash a window at the back. You get everything ready and we will go from there". Veronica whispered.

Kevin agreed and kissed her on the cheek as she left.

Evie appeared at the kitchen door and spotted me, "What are you doing Shirley?" she asked.

"Oh, I am just checking out the stonework" I replied and went back into the kitchen to tell Doris, very quietly, what I had just heard.

Aunt Kate looked at me. "I hope you are not planning anything Shirley. You look suspicious, I know that look."

I just laughed and denied everything.

We could hear Evie asking Kevin if he had managed to get her some insecticide for her rosebushes.

"Yes, it's in my study I will fetch it now," shouted Kevin.

Evie returned with the brown bag containing the small bottle, "I hope this works, my roses are covered with greenfly," said Evie.

Doris began to giggle, we doubted that it would, considering it was only peppermint essence. But it was better to be safe and we said nothing.

Evie and Aunt Kate walked out on to the patio with the so-called POISON and started putting it on the roses!

The rest of the day, we just hung around and watched television and countless films. We could not really concentrate on anything. I had a feeling of excitement, fear and sadness for Evie. I knew Doris felt exactly the same and at long last Doris asked the usual question, as I knew she would.

"Shirley, it's time we told somebody now and I know who to tell. On the original paper cutting of the theft in New York there is a telephone number asking for information. We can phone them."

That was a good idea but I was not quite ready yet. "That is a brilliant idea Doris, but let's just wait and see what happens on Tuesday. I promise that on Wednesday we will do it. We will know all the details by then". I said reassuringly.

Doris thought about it. "OK Shirley, but Wednesday is the day. I will not change my mind even if you try to distract me with talk of monks and tunnels. I know what you have been up to! But on Wednesday I will not be distracted. Are you listening Shirley?" Doris said with confidence.

I just agreed, knowing that she was right.

All day it continued to rain and the wind was really howling. We played a few board games and decided to have an early night.

We sat in bed and Doris got out her notebook and we added notes about Veronica and the operatic tickets and what she had said to Kevin about the Tuesday night expedition. Finally, we talked about the buried treasure and wondered what it was.

"I think it will make us all very rich and it will change our lives forever," said a hopeful Doris.

"Yes, maybe it will, but remember what the riddle said, we must give to the poor and needy," I instructed. I did not want her getting too excited, just to be disappointed.

Doris pulled a strange face and looked at me but she didn't say anything else except "Goodnight then."

Sunday lunch with Kevin was all we wanted, we were not in the least bit hungry, but we had to go through the ritual of dressing up and pretending to be really excited. Doris and I had phoned our parents and we were secretly wishing we were going home.

"Just a week left to go Shirley," said Doris.

"Yes, I know" I replied. I had to admit I was feeling homesick and had to tell myself not to be so silly. I had to be in control of my emotions and not show Doris that I was really quite scared, even though I am sure that underneath she knew already. Doris and I had a job to do and we had to see it through to the end, even though we knew there would be no happy ending.

We all got in the car and Kevin drove us to a rather posh looking restaurant that overlooked the sea. It had taken us about half an hour to get there. Aunt Kate had dressed to impress, wearing some of her new clothes that she had bought in St Peter's Port. Evie had worn the ruby necklace and her emerald bracelet, complimented by a yellow, floral dress. Doris and I had put on our party dresses from the other night, they were the only things we had with us except for jeans, and Kevin was wearing a black dinner suit. Doris and I could not help laughing because he looked like a penguin; he was not impressed with our giggling. Aunt Kate had been laughing too and he just stared at her. I suppose it was a bit rude but he did not deserve any better.

The food was fine and the lunch passed very quickly. Kevin was tipping the waiter every five minutes and the meal was finished off with a bottle of champagne. Doris had looked at the menu and told me, that particular bottle was priced at two hundred pounds! Well, he might be celebrating now, we thought, but it won't last long.

Eventually we left the restaurant and walked outside. The sun had come out but the wind was still blowing really hard. Kevin was standing there smoking a big cigar and the wind was blowing all the ash on his dinner jacket and his hair was blowing everywhere. He looked a complete mess; Evie was trying to brush off the cigar ash from his jacket. He threw the burnt-out cigar stub on the floor and started walking.

"Shall we walk along the cliffs?" he said and he headed for a small path that was narrow and right by the edge of the high cliffs. "It's supposed to be a lovely walk with some great views."

I looked at Doris and could feel a tight knot in my stomach and my heart was pounding. There was something wrong here. Why would he want us to walk so close to the edge of the cliffs when the wind was blowing so hard? Was this an attempt to get rid of Aunt Kate or maybe us?

"Do you mind if we go home now? I don't feel well," I said, my voice shaking.

Kevin stopped in his tracks and turned around and glared at me. "You're always ill. You can wait in the car," he said sharply and he threw me the car keys.

Just then Aunt Kate intervened, "I would rather go home too. We are not exactly dressed for a walk and these heels are killing me."

Kevin walked back to the car, snatching the keys out of my hand. "Please yourselves then," he muttered as he was climbing back into the car.

The drive home was a silent one and we could tell he was in a bad mood.

"What's the matter Shirley? Are you feeling ill?" enquired Doris quietly.

"No, I feel fine and I wanted to keep it that way, Kevin was up to something. Let's keep out of his way when we get home" I replied.

"Good idea". Doris said.

We didn't have to worry he went straight into his study and we didn't have to see him the rest of the day. But we did hear him and Evie bickering in the kitchen after we went to bed.

Chapter 13 - Planning, preparation and action

It was Monday morning and I couldn't help thinking about our usual Monday routine at home. Dad and Mum would be having their breakfasts and Mum would be shouting me from the hall telling me to hurry up. Dad would leave for work and would always be whistling the same tune as he walked down the path. I would go to my window and he'd wave to me from the garden gate. Mum and I always leave the house together and she would walk with me to catch the school bus and then hurry off to work.

Oh, I did miss that normal life. I would sit by Doris on the bus and we would catch up on what had been happening and plan our week. Sometimes we would read the crime reports from our local paper and decide if our help was needed. Now, when I say crime, that could mean a missing cat or somebody losing their pension book. Not a lot ever happened, but it kept my mystery solving brain in gear. However, here we were, in the middle of a real situation that could go horribly wrong. I was really enjoying the challenge, but I felt sad for Evie.

We had already solved the mystery of the riddle and the tunnel and how the monks were making their money from the sale of elicit alcohol so we had that to be proud of, but now it was time to unveil how horrible Kevin and Veronica really were.

The rest of the day was put to what we called "planning and preparation" and it involved looking at all the facts and preparing everything that we needed for tomorrow night's antics. We charged up both our phones and had also found a couple of torches and some spare batteries in the garage. We mixed up some mud and water so that we could smear it on our faces to act as camouflage and found ourselves some dark coloured clothing. We even practised running from one end of the garden to the other to help our running speeds for the long run back up the tunnel that we would be doing tomorrow evening to check out what exactly was happening at the jewellery shop. We were ready for everything we could possibly think about. I always believed that careful planning was the answer to all mystery solving solutions and, of course, a sharp, logical mind. Doris had an eye for detail. What could possibly go wrong?

At some point in the day Veronica had arrived to give Evie the opera tickets and she had brought us the movie to watch '101 Dalmatians'. Did she realise how old we were? It was a good film when we were about six but we were hoping for a mystery film or a rom-com. The only good thing about it was that it made Doris and I laugh thinking about Veronica's striking resemblance to Cruella de Ville.

"Why are you girls laughing so much?" she asked.

"No reason" we replied.

Suddenly, with great force, she threw two packs of popcorn at us "Try not to choke" she said. I think she liked us as much as we liked her.

She invited Aunt Kate and Evie to have a makeover in her salon the next morning, they agreed and then she left, with Evie following her down the hall.

Aunt Kate looked at both of us. "Now girls you could have said goodbye to her. Have you lost your manners?" she said with disappointment in her voice.

If only she knew what was going on she would not have said that. However, we could not tell her yet.

"Sorry" we replied and continued with our planning.

Kevin was going in and out all day but did not once speak to us. We did not really care. By six o'clock we were all ready and decided to relax the rest of the day. We ate lots of snacks to maintain our strength. This was where I differed from Sherlock Holmes, he didn't seem to eat much, but I suppose he smoked his pipe instead. I knew which I preferred and, in his day, things were very different.

Tuesday morning arrived and we both woke up early.

"Well Shirley, today is the day that we have been waiting for. I feel a bit nervous about it. Do you?" said Doris as she rubbed her eyes and slowly got out of bed.

"Yes, I do feel a bit nervous but nothing can go wrong. We are organised. We just have to stay calm and follow the plan." I replied.

Doris nodded her head and said, "Let's get some breakfast".

After breakfast we headed down to the town. Evie and Aunt Kate went to Veronica's salon and Doris and I looked around the town. We checked out the Monk's Head pub, went around the back into the car park to make sure that there was nothing on top of our escape route and we double-checked our timings. It was exactly two minutes from the jewellery shop.

"Great, let's get back to the square and meet Evie and Aunt Kate," I said.

We sat on the bench in the middle and waited for them to emerge. When they eventually appeared, they were both plastered in makeup and looking very different.

"You look more like my sister instead of my mother," joked Evie to Aunt Kate.

This had delighted Aunt Kate but I must say Doris and I thought they both looked ten years older, but obviously we did not say this. We were not impressed with Veronica's makeup artistry, but we wouldn't be, we disliked her so much.

After having coffee and cake we headed back home. The afternoon seemed to drag on but after an early tea Aunt Kate and Evie went to get ready for their night out.

Kevin had returned from work and was busy setting up the DVD player in the lounge when we went in to sit down. He had placed two bowls of popcorn and some drinks on the coffee table.

At six thirty a taxi came to collect Evie and Aunt Kate and Kevin walked them to the door.

"Have a good time and don't rush back. Have a nice meal after the show I will be here to look after the girls. We will be fine," he said, reassuringly.

Doris and I had just managed to hide our bag of clothes and mud mixture behind the curtain, when Kevin walked in. He insisted on switching on the film for us and told us he would be in his study if we needed anything.

"OK" we replied and pretended to watch the film.

Seven o'clock arrived and still nothing had happened.

"Had we got the facts right?" I asked Doris.

Just before she could answer we heard the old phone ring in the hall way and Kevin picked it up and we heard him talking.

We opened the door so that we could hear what was going on.

"Hello Ben, What's that? The alarm has gone off? Oh dear, Evie is here but she has laryngitis and can't say a word. Yes, she does have the keys and the other half of the code. Don't worry Ben, I will bring her down to the shop but she will not be able to talk to you. See you in ten minutes" and then Kevin put down the phone.

We had been listening at the door but jumped back on the sofa when we heard Kevin approaching. "Girls, I will have to go out for half an hour. Will you be all right? Don't mention it to Evie or I will be in big trouble! You are both grown up enough, aren't you?" he said with a raised tone in his voice.

"Yes, we will be fine Kevin we are really enjoying this film" we replied and Kevin headed for his study, picked up his briefcase and hurriedly left, got in his car and drove down the drive.

Now we had to leap into action.

"QUICK Doris, put the old clothes over the top of our proper clothes and let's smear each other's faces with the mud mixture. Grab your phone and the torches and let's head down the tunnel. We must stick the film on hold so that it is ready for when we get back."

We headed for the garden and entered the tunnel in the usual manner and then jumped in the cart; this time it was easier with the torch and we did not have to use the brakes as much as last time because we knew where we were going. We were hurtling down at a really fast speed and our hair was blowing everywhere, but we didn't care. Suddenly, we could see the wooden door and we both pulled really hard on the brake. The cart stopped quickly but this time we were ready and we didn't get flung out. Yes, everything was going to plan. Before entering the pub, we peeped around the door to make sure there was nobody in the cellar, we were in luck and so we clambered up the wooden steps into the car park and we rushed around the front of the pub.

We had to hide in a doorway when we saw Kevin drive past. He stopped outside the jewellery shop and guess who was with him? It was Veronica dressed, of course, to look like Evie. She wore her long red wig and she even had one of Evie's dresses on.

Ben the short-sighted security guard was waiting by the door and we could hear the alarm going off and see a blue light flashing from just above the shop.

"Come on Doris let's get closer, we cannot hear what is being said," I said.

We both rushed across the road and hid behind a small wall that adjoined the shop. Ben put in his alarm code followed by Veronica who was waving her arms around as if doing sign language and pretending she couldn't talk. When I say Veronica's code, I mean Evie's. Kevin must have stolen it, and the key, from Evie's handbag that she had hidden in her wardrobe for safekeeping.

The alarm had now stopped and Kevin was giving them both instructions. "I will stay out here, but if I were you Ben I would search upstairs and Evie should search downstairs. Be careful and take your time."

We watched Kevin hand Veronica a set of keys and she and Ben both went inside. Kevin just stood there walking backwards and forwards outside the doorway.

Ten minutes later Ben and Veronica came out of the door.

"Everything is fine, I checked the camera when we first got in and could see nothing, but there is a broken window on the first floor. Some kids must have thrown a stone through it and triggered the alarm. Thank you, Evie, for coming and I hope you're better soon" said Ben as he was locking up the door.

Veronica patted Ben on the back and just waved to him as she and Kevin were walking away.

With Ben gone and nobody else about, Kevin began to speak to Veronica. "Well how did it go?" he asked nervously.

"Like a dream, the silly old fool can't see anything. I had plenty of time to open the cabinet and make the swap and I made sure the camera caught me doing all of it. Evie will be their main suspect and, by the time they find out she is innocent, we will be sipping champagne on a beach somewhere; poor, little, stupid Evie," Veronica mocked.

Kevin just laughed and Veronica handed him the keys.

"Now, tomorrow I will go to the bank and do that transfer. It's a bit risky; there must be something wrong with Evie's passport. I will meet you in my office at four o'clock and we can both go in to the bank. It looks more convincing. Remember, do not wear that dress, put on that long coat I gave you; I bought Evie the same one," instructed Kevin.

Then something fell suddenly out of the wall that we were hiding behind and Veronica stared directly at us.

"RUN!" I said and we both ran across the road and around the back of the Monks Head.

We could hear Veronica running after us and saying, "Kevin it's them horrible girls! Quickly let's get them."

Our running practices in the garden paid off and we were down the trap door and back in the pub cellar before Veronica and Kevin had turned the corner. We stood in the darkness the only sound we could hear was our hearts beating. Kevin was standing right on top of the trapdoor.

"Veronica, don't be so stupid. The girls are at home I saw them just before I left. It's not possible. It's just kids playing; now come on let's get out of here. It's your imagination," and we could hear them walking away.

"Come on Doris, let's carry on with our plan. Are you ready for our big run up that tunnel? We have got to be there before Kevin returns or the game will be up and who knows what will happen then." I said taking deep breaths to get myself ready.

"Let's go then," said Doris and we set off. Now we both took a deep breath and held hands and began our marathon up the tunnel. The tunnel seemed longer than usual and because it had been raining it was really slippery, but we kept on going.

Doris suddenly screamed. "There are two rats straight in front of us. I hate rats!"

"Never mind them they are more scared of you; just keep running. Kevin is the only rat to be scared of." I said trying to reassure her.

I gripped her hand tighter and we continued. The rats were running in all directions and I was glad when we eventually reached the part of the tunnel that branched off and it levelled out. We kept on going and reached the steps, opened up the door and climbed out on to the grass. Doris who was really out of breath sat down on the grass gasping for air.

"No time to rest now let's get back into the lounge". I said pulling her up and coaxing her to move faster. In the distance we could see Kevin driving up the drive and we rushed into the lounge, took off our outer clothes that were plastered in mud and wiped off the mud from our faces. As we sat down, we put the film back on and each of us grabbed a bowl of popcorn. With seconds to spare Kevin walked in.

He had a big grin on his face as if he was really proud of what he had just done. "Are you girls enjoying the film? I am going back into my study now but if you need anything give me a shout and, by the way, remember not to tell Evie and Aunt Kate that I slipped out or you will be in real trouble" he said in a type of joking way, but we think he meant it.

"Yes, OK," we replied and he left the room and we both breathed a sigh of relief.

"Not much time to spare there was there Shirley? We only just made it. You and your bright ideas. What would have happened if Veronica had caught us?" said Doris in panic mode.

"Look, we made it and Veronica didn't catch us. She cannot prove that it was us. Just calm down Doris, now we know exactly what is happening and what their treacherous plan is". I replied. It had been a lucky escape but we had done it.

"Yes, I guess you're right Shirley, but it was scary, wasn't it? And now we can tell the police all the facts tomorrow. Ben the security guard was not much good at his job, was he? That's probably why Mr Fairbanks has kept him!" said Doris.

I agreed, but couldn't help thinking about Miss Blackly, she had seemed very efficient, was she in on the crime too? Surely, she would notice that her most expensive pieces were fake.

The so-called plan was that nobody discovered the robbery until Monday, when Mr Fairbanks was back from his holiday. Kevin and Veronica would be going away on Friday taking all the genuine pieces of jewellery with them and all of the jewels from the New York raid. Mr Fairbanks would claim his insurance money and poor old Ben and Evie would be under great suspicion. There were still some questions I could not answer: Why would Kevin and Veronica wait this long to cash in their first haul of jewels? And why would they bother with the jewellery shop? Maybe they were just both so greedy and so very cruel!

There was a noise in the hall and we heard the front door bang close, it was Aunt Kate and Evie returning from their night out. Aunt Kate was busy singing some dreadful song and Evie was laughing. We walked into the hall. Aunt Kate had obviously enjoyed the performance and was singing loudly.

My Mum was the same, you could tell they were sisters. It made me feel homesick again. However, the singing sounded a bit like a cat's choir (that's what Dad would have called it anyway). Kevin came out of his study and insisted on making them a cup of tea.

Doris and I had got really tired probably after all the excitement and all that running and decided to go to bed. We could not stand to watch Kevin be so slimy when we knew exactly what a horrible person he was.

Chapter 14 - Doris gets her wish

The next day, Doris had charged her phone and we went into the bedroom. We got out the notebook and Doris phoned the American number on the newspaper cutting. We must have spoken to at least three departments until we eventually spoke to someone who took us seriously. We put the phone on speakerphone so that we could both speak and hear what was going on. Between the two of us we told them everything from the wedding, the teddy bear, the machinery in Veronica's salon shed and all the notes we had written in the notebook and the tunnel that had helped us to witness what had happened last night.

At last, the policeman on the other end of the phone said "Now girls you must listen and obey what I say. The man and woman you are talking about are not Kevin Richman and Veronica Richman they are Brad Poorman and Vera Dross and they are very dangerous, wanted criminals. They have so many different names and so many different passports that we have been unable to catch them. They have done crimes like these many times before and Brad has been married several times and has taken his so-called wives' money. They are both very dangerous and would think nothing of getting you two out of the way. You must leave everything to us now and do not tell anyone and do not upset them. Are you listening?"

Doris and I had no choice but to agree and we put the phone down. We were both shocked we knew they were horrible but could not guess just how horrible they were.

"I feel so much better now do you, Shirley?" said Doris.

I thought about my answer. "Yes, I do Doris you were right, it had to be done and they will deal with everything now. They will inform the bank straight away and when Kevin and Veronica get there this afternoon Evie's account will be blocked. Do you know Doris; we have worked out everything for the police and I think we should be really proud of ourselves for solving this crime. Let's go and get a milkshake to celebrate," I replied feeling very proud.

We ran down the stairs into the kitchen and took our drinks out on to the patio and sat on two reclining chairs.

Doris, who had hiccups from drinking too fast, asked, "When can we dig up the hidden treasure?"

"Soon, very soon but let's get them two safely behind bars and then we can tell everybody". I replied.

The sun was warm and I think the relief of leaving it up to the police had made us both feel relaxed and we both drifted off to sleep. A familiar voice woke us up.

"Hi girls." We opened our eyes and there was Veronica standing right in front of us. She was wittering on in that terrible tone of hers "Did you enjoy the movie last night. Them poor little kittens, they nearly drowned didn't they. No loss if they did, I hate kittens and cats."

We both sat up and Doris, who I think was still half asleep, muttered. "The film was called 101 Dalmatians. They are obviously dogs not cats and the woman in it was called Cruella de Ville. We hated her and she so reminds us of someone, all that makeup and stupid accent."

Veronica just grinned and walked through the library into the kitchen.

"That was a very brave answer, Doris. I think she was testing us about last night's antics, but you put her straight. Well done, Doris". I said and we both laughed.

Doris was impressed and I think she was glad that she was half asleep, she had not thought about her answer too hard and she was proud of her bravery.

Evie and Aunt Kate were in the kitchen making dinner and we heard Veronica ask if Kevin was in his study. She walked over to the study door.

"Open up Kevin, it's me and I need to speak to you," she shouted.

Kevin opened the door and let her in. It had become second nature to follow and listen and so we hid under the stairwell and listened to their conversation even though we had been told not to.

"Is everything ready? Have you fuelled up the boat? We will go to the bank later on; I will meet you at four. Why have you come here anyway?" asked Kevin.

"Everything is ready, I just came to check up on them girls. I was sure I saw them last night but I must have got it wrong. Soon we will be away from this awful place and them nauseating girls and them two ugly witches," Veronica replied.

What a cheek, we thought, there was only one witch here and we knew all too well who that was. Then she came out of the study and walked back into the kitchen. Evie and Aunt Kate thanked her for the opera tickets and asked if she would like to come over later for her dinner.

"No, thank you, I don't like your British cuisine." and on that note, she turned around and walked out.

At three o'clock Kevin left and, of course, we knew where he was going. We hoped that the bank had been informed and that they had blocked their joint account. Doris and I decided to go for a walk and left Evie and Aunt Kate in the kitchen having a cup of tea. A couple of hours later we saw Kevin driving up the drive.

"Let's go and see what sort of mood he is in now," said Doris and we rushed back into the kitchen. In walked Kevin looking really flustered and annoyed.

"What's the matter with you?" asked Evie.

"Nothing" he replied and marched into his study banging the door behind him.

Doris and I smiled at each other. Oh dear, the bank must have refused him access to his account. Evie had decided that tomorrow we would go on some more trips around the area. We hoped that Kevin would be too busy to go, fingers crossed. At least he didn't join us for dinner.

"He had a terrible headache," Evie informed us.

At breakfast, Kevin announced that he was too busy to come on our trip. We tried not to look too pleased.

Just then, the post arrived and Kevin went to collect it from the hallway. "There's one here for you Evie," he said and handed her the letter.

She sat down and opened it at the table and read it carefully. "That's strange it's from the passport office, they are confirming that my passport has been cancelled because I have lost it and a new one will be sent soon. You have my passport don't you Kevin? I know nothing about this," said Evie handing the letter back to Kevin for him to check it.

Doris went really red and she didn't know where to look.

Kevin, who was looking directly at Doris, noticed her nervousness. "What's the matter with you? Do you girls know anything about this?" He asked bluntly. His face was getting redder and redder and his voice was getting louder and louder. He looked as if he was going to burst.

"Stop being silly it must be a mistake. I will phone them tomorrow and find out," interrupted Evie.

Thank goodness for that. I could see that Doris was at breaking point.

I got up and grabbed Doris by the hand. "Come on Doris let's go and get ready for our trip," I said and pulled her to her feet. I could tell her hands were shaking and I had to get her upstairs before she fainted.

We sat on the bed. "Calm down, Doris, we only have a day to go and then it will all be over. Are you OK? I said softly.

"Yes, I am fine. I am sorry Shirley, but he was looking straight at me and I just panicked," Doris replied.

Once Doris had settled down, we got ready for our trip and went downstairs and kept out of his way until we got into the car with Evie and Aunt Kate.

The day soon passed. It was a lovely day and we visited a few museums and then strolled some beautiful gardens overlooking the sea. I think Evie said they were called 'Candie Gardens'. We had our lunch sitting on a bench. It was lovely to just relax and not worry about seeing Kevin.

When we returned home the house was empty and we enjoyed homemade pizza and watched television together. When Doris and I went to bed we decided not to chat; we would need all our wits about us tomorrow.

Chapter 15 - The Dreaded Day

The day had eventually arrived, but we still didn't know what was going to happen. We woke early and chatted for a bit then went downstairs for breakfast. Kevin was rushing around here, there and everywhere. All his bags were in the hall.

Aunt Kate was sitting by the table. "Good morning, it's like a madhouse here. Get your breakfast and sit down quickly or he will pack you two. He is only going for a few days. What on earth does he want all this stuff for? You would think that he is going forever," said Aunt Kate.

We did not answer, but we could hear furniture being dragged about in his study.

Evie came into the kitchen and her eyes were red as if she had been crying.

"Are you alright?" asked Aunt Kate.

"Yes, it must be the pollen in the garden," replied Evie and she made herself a drink of hot chocolate.

Just then, there was a knock at the door; it was Veronica, "Is he ready yet?" she asked.

"Yes, I think so, but you don't have to bother, I can take him to the airport. There is no need for you to do it," replied Evie.

"Don't talk nonsense, you have enough to do here with all these waifs and strays," replied Veronica smugly.

This made Evie and Aunt Kate very angry, but before they could say anything Kevin came out of his study and everybody went through the ritual of saying goodbye with the usual hugs and kisses. Doris and I stood well back; we did not want any part of that.

When all of the luggage was in the car Kevin ran back into his study and brought out an even bigger briefcase than usual and he got into the car looking really happy.

He shouted out of the car window, "See you all, maybe, be lucky!"

"See you, Brad. I don't think so!" shouted Doris.

Aunt Kate heard her. "What did you just say, Doris? Who is Brad?" she asked looking bewildered.

Doris stuttered, and said, "I meant, how sad."

"Oh, I see," said Aunt Kate.

I could not help thinking that his LUCK had just run out.

We all went to sit on the patio and had pancakes with maple syrup. They were divine and it took our minds off the day's events.

"What do you think will happen now Shirley," asked Doris.

"I don't know, but I am sure we will hear shortly" I replied.

At twelve o'clock there was another knock at the door and Evie went to open it. I couldn't believe my eyes; walking onto the patio was Dad and Mum.

I ran up to them and gave them a big hug "What are you doing here? I asked.

"I have finished Mum's kitchen and fancied a few days away and we thought we would give you all a surprise. Your mother loves her kitchen so much; she does not want to cook in it. So, I thought I would try some Guernsey cooking," said Dad jokingly.

Aunt Kate and Evie were as excited as me and tea and cakes were brought onto the patio.

"Come on girls, let them chat. You can show me around this old house," said Dad.

We walked into the library. Dad shut the patio doors behind him. This, I thought, was suspicious; he would not have done that unless he had something important to say. I looked at him and waited.

I did not have to wait long.

"Shirley, I have had a phone call from the American police department and I know everything. So does your mother. That's the real reason we have come. Your Mum and Dad know as well, Doris. Why on earth did you both not tell anyone? You could have been in so much danger," said Dad harshly.

I looked across at Doris and I could see tears running down her face.

Dad had noticed as well, "Look you have done a good thing and you're not in trouble but we were all worried about you both. Shirley, you should have told me."

"I am sorry Dad, but we were not sure and had to find out properly. If we had told anyone they would not have believed us anyway. We made sure that everything was done logically and safely just like Sherlock Holmes would have done," I replied.

Dad started to smile, "You read too many books and watch too much television. You must realise that sometimes real-life is not like that. I know you cannot resist interfering in things; you must take after your mother." He said, shaking his head. "Well, all right, you are both safe that's the main thing. The police are going to follow Kevin and Veronica until they reach Paris. They will arrest them there and then hopefully they will be able to get the dealer as well. Until then, we just have to wait, but the local police will come this evening and tell Evie and Aunt Kate. Your mother is not going to say anything until then and she will be here to help. They are going to have a terrible shock and that kettle will be working flat out with all those cups of tea. We will leave them all chatting. But I want to know all about this so-called riddle and tunnel and, of course, the treasure," Dad replied in his usual tone.

We showed him everything: the monk's bible, the riddle, the picture in the library and explained how we managed to open the tunnel.

"Right, I have heard enough let's grab a shovel and find that hidden treasure," he said with excitement.

We grabbed our phones and torch and marched across to the sundial. Dad brought the biggest shovel he could find and I could tell he was very excited, as were we.

"What is going on?" asked Evie and we told her.

"Doris and I have found the secret tunnel and there is treasure in it."

They quickly got up from the seats and followed us over to the sundial.

Doris and I went through the motions and entered the tunnel with everybody following close behind. We showed them the copper barrels and all the bottles and we walked down the tunnel that led to the coast. It took us ages and Aunt Kate waited halfway down, as her shoes were not really suitable.

When we reached the bottom, Dad peeped through the hole in the rocks but decided he was not going to fit. We returned to Aunt Kate who was holding the torch and looking terrified.

"Don't worry there is only a couple of rats who live here," said Doris.

That seemed to make Aunt Kate look even more frightened, "Doris you are not really helping," she said.

We all laughed and Evie and Mum helped Aunt Kate back up the tunnel. We all walked down the other branch of the tunnel but did not go into the Monks Head.

"Right, where is this treasure hidden then?" Dad asked.

We walked up to the carving of the bell on the wall and they all read the riddle. Dad rolled up his sleeves and started digging. Doris was doing the nervous leg shuffle and it seemed to take forever and then Dad hit something solid, it sounded like a wooden box.

"I've got it!" Dad shouted. We all waited in anticipation as he dragged the box out of the ground. It was plastered with mud and it took some time to clean it off the top. With the phones and the torch pointing at it, Dad opened the box. We all peered in. We could see four bottles, a book and twelve little blue bags that were filled to the brim with gold-coloured coins.

"Are they real gold? I asked.

"I don't know," said Dad.

The bottles looked ancient and were filled with some liquid and we presumed it was their brewed alcohol. The old book seemed to be a diary and there were names and ages of all the monks and a record of all the money they had got.

"Wow, we should phone the local history society they will be so grateful and they will know what to do next," Mum said with excitement.

We all agreed and decided not to touch anything else and we all left the tunnel and Dad found their telephone number and phoned them.

Within an hour they had turned up, bringing the harbour master with them. They were all very excited and we were instructed to keep out of the way.

Doris was furious with their attitude, "That's gratitude for you. If it wasn't for us, Shirley, they would not have found it would they?" she said.

"I know Doris, but that's how things go; they need to list and classify everything first and then they will tell you what is happening," I said, trying to reassure her.

The rest of the day they were going in and out of the tunnel and eventually they cordoned the tunnel off and stuck a padlock on it.

At about seven o'clock it all went quiet and we got a quick snack for dinner.

Dad kept looking at his watch and checking his phone for messages and then there was a knock on the door.

Dad got up from the table "I'll go". He said in a nervous voice.

Standing by the door were three police officers and they went into the lounge; Dad instructed Doris and me to wait outside in the kitchen and took everybody else into the lounge. He shut the door behind him. They must have talked for about fifteen minutes. We could hear crying and suddenly Evie ran past us up the stairs and we heard her bedroom door slam shut.

Mum was busy trying to calm down Aunt Kate and Dad came to speak to us. "It's all over now girls. Kevin and Veronica have been arrested and they also got the dealer. They were caught red-handed with all the jewellery including the Burmese Bloodstone necklace and lots of other jewellery they had stolen over many years. The police said there were millions and millions of pounds worth. The police were very pleased, girls, with all your hard work and detective skills."

"Can we do anything to help Dad?" I asked.

"Why not make some strong tea for everyone, that always makes things better," came his reply. We made the tea and took it into the lounge.

Aunt Kate looked dreadful and Mum was still trying to calm her down. "I will take a cup up to Evie," said Mum and left the room.

"Oh, girls this is terrible. What you two have gone through, you're very brave. I knew there was something wrong with him, but he was a very good actor. Shirley, I am so glad your Mum and Dad are here, I would not be able to cope," said poor Aunt Kate.

We just nodded and Dad came back into the room.

Doris and I decided to go into our bedroom and keep out of the way until the shock had worn off.

Not long afterwards Mum came into our room with drinks and cake and sat on the bed talking to us.

"This is awful," said Doris.

"Yes, it is, but it had to be found out at some point and its better for Evie to find out now. She will be fine; she is broken-hearted but things will get better and before long she will be back to her usual self. It's just a lesson in life that sometimes we all have to learn. Now, eat your cake and get a goodnight sleep, tomorrow will be a new day. Goodnight," said Mum hugging us both and then she left the room.

I was so glad that Dad and Mum had arrived. How would we have coped?

Chapter 16 - Going back home

When we woke, we could hear a lot of noise coming from the garden. There were around twenty people all standing in a circle talking, the historical society was back with the Mayor who was dressed in his finery. We got dressed and ran downstairs and could see Dad talking to a couple of police officers by the tunnel entrance.

When he saw us, he came across, "The police have told us to say nothing about the crimes as they still want to catch Mr Fairbanks, so not a word to anyone," he said.

"OK, we will not say a word. How are Evie and Aunt Kate?" we asked.

"They will be fine," Dad replied.

The mayor came over to us and handed us a large key. "This is the key to the town. It is to say thank you for finding the tunnel and the hidden treasure. You can do and have anything you like with our gratitude," said the mayor.

Doris was thrilled that they had appreciated what we had done. "Were the coins real gold?" she asked.

"Oh yes, they were and they are worth a fortune. The owner of the priory has given permission for you two to decide what you want to do with them?" he said smiling at us.

Doris and I had a small discussion and we both decided to do what the riddle had said and went back to the mayor. "We will give it to the poor and needy, maybe build a hospice or hospital," came our reply.

The mayor looked delighted and once again thanked us.

Dad looked very proud of us and put his arms around us. "Well done, your Mums will be so very proud of you. Now go and get ready we are heading down the town for a slap-up meal. I am starving!" Dad said, rubbing his stomach.

Mum came with us and dad did a lot of eating and we shopped for gifts with Mum. When we got back the garden was quiet and Evie and Aunt Kate were sitting out on the patio. They had both calmed down and we showed them what we had bought.

Evie stood up and looked directly at Doris and me. "Thank you. I knew things were not right but I did not realise how wrong things really were," she said.

"Evie, we are really sorry to hurt you" we replied and we did not mention it again.

The next day was spent packing up Evie's things; she had decided to travel back home with us. There was no reason for her to stay in St Peters port any longer. Monday arrived and Dad packed everything into his car.

"Do we have everything? We had better hurry if are going to catch that ferry," he asked.

"I will go and check" I replied. I ran upstairs and I could see Evie sitting on her bed clutching the little teddy bear with his red heart, she looked very sad. I sat down on the bed with her.

"Do you remember Evie, when I was little and I cried or if something had really upset me you would always say 'Things will be better tomorrow. When you feel that your heart has broken, it never really has and the tears that you cry act like glue and stick that cracked heart back together and next time it will be stronger'" I said really quietly. I did not usually go in for all that slushy stuff but, sometimes, it was needed.

She wiped her tears, smiled and put her arm around my shoulders, "I don't remember saying that, Shirley, but it's right. I will become a much stronger person after this and, if I said it, then it's definitely a fact" she replied.

She got up from the bed and placed the teddy bear on her dressing table with all the fake jewellery that she had and we left the room, shutting the door behind us. I think I heard the little bear fall on the floor as we left, it didn't matter anymore anyway.

The sea crossing was really rough and we were so glad to get back to the port. Poor Aunt Kate had been seasick as if she hadn't already had a rough time of it.

Eventually, we arrived back home in Dashington and we were so glad. Doris's parents were waiting for us and Doris was so pleased to see them.

Life from then on carried on as normal.

Six months later we heard that Kevin and Veronica had been jailed for twenty-five years and Mr Fairbanks jailed for ten years. It turned out that Miss Blackly had been sent on some course and had nothing to do with the crime.

The monk's tunnel had been opened up to the public and the money was been used for the seaman's mission. The gold coins had been sold to a museum and the funds used to build a hospice for ill people. They would be opening it next year and Doris and I have been invited to cut the blue ribbon. Dad has been sent a bottle of the monk's brew and he says that he is keeping it for Christmas. Mum thinks it would be best suited for cleaning the drains, but we will see.

Last week Doris and I were awarded a certificate from the American government to say "Thank you". We have also received two diamond rings from the jewellery shop in New York. Doris and I decided that we'd had enough of jewellery and gave them to our Mums.

Evie has slowly got back to normal and started a new job and loves it. Every month we go shopping with her and each time she seems to get better.

There was one question I still had no answer to. Who's last will had Kevin been busy studying?

Dad had asked the police, "It was the Last Will and Testimony of Vera Dross and it left everything to Kevin or, should I say, Brad Poorman. Apparently, Vera had never seen it and definitely never signed it."

I couldn't help thinking what Kevin was going to do with her; maybe it was lucky for her that she had been arrested.

Mrs Dukkas from the post office is always asking questions about the whole thing, but to her annoyance, we tell her we are working for the American government and cannot tell her anything. Which really makes us smile.

Of course, Doris has told Miles Drakeford the whole story and he thinks she is a real hero.

Aunt Kate is fine now and has given us five hundred pounds each for saving all of Evie's money.

In all, the whole thing was a complete success. It has made Doris and I realise that when we get older, we want to be private detectives. Even now, the phone keeps ringing and we discover many mysteries in the world that need our HELP.

Remember to watch this space.

THE END.

Printed in Great Britain
by Amazon